CENTER FIELD

ALSO BY
ROBERT LIPSYTE

ROBERT LIPSYTE

CENTER FIELD

HARPER TEEN

An Imprint of HarperCollins*Publishers*

HarperTeen is an imprint of HarperCollins Publishers.

Center Field

Library of Congress Cataloging-in-Publication Data
Lipsyte, Robert.
    Center field / Robert Lipsyte. — 1st ed.
      p. cm.
    Summary: Mike lives for baseball and hopes to follow his idol into
the major leagues one day, but he is distracted by a new player who
might take his place in center field, an ankle injury, problems at
home, and a growing awareness that something sinister is happening
at school.
    ISBN 978-0-06-055704-1 (trade bdg.)
    ISBN 978-0-06-055705-8 (lib. bdg.)
    [1. Baseball—Fiction. 2. Conduct of life—Fiction. 3. High
schools—Fiction. 4. Schools—Fiction. 5. Identity—Fiction.
6. Family life—New Jersey—Fiction. 7. New Jersey—Fiction.]
I. Title.
PZ7.L67Cen 2010   2009014586
[Fic]—dc22   CIP
                                                         AC

Typography by Andrea Vandergrift
10 11 12 13 14   LP/RRDB   10 9 8 7 6 5 4 3 2 1

First Edition

For my newest teammates,
Alfred and Sylvia

PART ONE

"I try as hard in spring training as in the World Series. You have to practice to win."
—*IMs to a Young Baller* by Billy Budd

ONE

Mike backed up at the *ping* of the ball against the metal bat, sensing a long, high fly. He felt a flush of joy. He was exactly where he wanted to be, in the center of the universe, racing a baseball, sure he was going to win.

The ball was rising. He turned and ran to the edge of the outfield grass, tracking it over his left shoulder. He judged the arc, decided it had reached the top. He stopped and focused on the ball as it fell against the bright blue sky. It briefly lost shape against a scrap of cloud, reappeared. Gotcha, he thought.

But it rose again on a puff of wind. He took a breath and sprinted for the outfield fence. He heard his spikes crunch on the running track. He'd slam into the fence if he didn't pull up.

Go for it, he thought. Coach is watching.

He heard his best friend, Ryan, huffing over from right

field yelling, "Fence!"

Thanks anyway.

Mike kicked out his right leg and hit the metal fence with the sole of his right shoe. He'd practiced this. His spikes hung on the web of wires long enough for him to boost himself straight up. He lost sight of the ball as he stretched his left arm, then heard the slap of leather, felt that good little sting. Got it. He squeezed the ball in his glove as his spikes scraped free and he slammed into the fence face-first. Then he fell back to earth. Never got that part right.

Ryan reached his left arm under him to break the fall. He still hit the ground hard. The bad right ankle yelped but Mike made no sound.

"Numbnuts," said Ryan, standing over him. He held out his hand. "Save it for real games."

Mike took his hand and pulled himself up. "Gotta practice to win."

"Gotta practice to break your ass."

"That, too." They laughed. Mike flipped the ball to Ryan, who spun and fired it home on one bounce. The catcher tossed it to the pitcher. Mike looked for Coach Cody. Didn't see him. Had Coach missed my catch?

The ankle sent tiny electric shocks up to Mike's shin as he trotted back to center field. Don't limp, he reminded himself. Don't give Coach any reason not to start you in

center field on opening day. You've been waiting for this all
your life.

He pushed past the pain to concentrate. Have to antici-
pate the ball quicker, especially if the ankle slows me down,
he thought. Got to ice the ankle when I get home. He'd
hurt it toward the end of football season but just wrapped it
tight and kept going. The football coach didn't consider you
hurt until a bone came through your skin.

Mike wondered if Coach Cody had noticed him hob-
bling on the football field. The baseball coach came to all
the football games even though he didn't like his baseball
starters to play any other sport. I wasn't one of his regular
starters then, thought Mike. That's going to change. Can't
wait until Coach announces the opening-day lineup next
week. Nobody at Ridgedale High plays center field better
than I do.

Except for the ankle, he felt good, loose and strong. The
team was shaping up. Ridgedale had won half its preseason
games, a pretty good record considering that Coach kept
shuffling the lineup and switching pitchers to get a look at
everybody. But Mike had started every game in center field.
This is going to be my season, he thought.

He imagined a day in June, three months from now,
springy green grass and soft earth under his spikes, the sun
cooking the hairs on the back of his neck, when a deep fly

would settle into his glove for the final out of the championship game.

Ridgedale wins!

Mike Semak awarded most valuable player trophy!

Billy Budd always said that visualizing success was the first step to achieving it. Billy should know. Starting center fielder for the world championship Yankees, last year's most valuable player in the World Series.

"Mine!" yelled Eric Nola in left field. He was dancing under a high fly.

Mike circled to back up Eric, a big senior with a live bat but a dead glove. He was slow, too. Mike could cover the shaky outfielder, and Coach knew it. Without Mike in center, Eric couldn't stay in the lineup.

Eric caught the easy fly. He juggled it, but held on, grinning with relief.

"Way to go, Eric," yelled Mike. It's more important to encourage guys when they do good than criticize them when they mess up. He'd read that in Billy Budd's book, too.

Concentrate now. Watch the batter's stance, the pitch, the swing, the sound off the bat. Follow the rock through the air right into your glove.

He checked where everybody was playing and moved forward a few steps. With his speed, he could afford to play shallow enough to catch bloopers and shut down grounders that got through the infield. He glanced at his friends, big Ryan in right and lanky, redheaded Andy at first base. Ryan would probably start, too. He was a long ball hitter and a solid fielder with a powerful arm. Be tougher for Andy, who was a streaky hitter and only a fair fielder. There was a hustling sophomore behind him on the depth chart who'd been having a good preseason. And sometimes Mike thought Andy didn't care as much about the game as he and Ryan did. Andy hated to run and lift with them, and he'd rather watch Fox News than ESPN, argue politics instead of talk ball.

Mike zoned into the next two batters. The scrimmage against Old Tappan was winding down. Both coaches were using it as more of a teaching exercise than a game since the teams weren't in the same conference. They would never meet this season in a real game.

With two outs, the Old Tappan batter punched a grounder to second and little Hector Ortiz gobbled it up and fired to Andy, who caught it to end the game. But the team captain, Todd Ganz, screamed at Andy from shortstop. Andy had apparently almost missed stepping on the bag. He held up his mitt to Todd so you could imagine the raised finger inside. Got to talk to Andy about his attitude, Mike thought.

TWO

The Ridgedale team began to trot in to high-five the Old Tappan players, but Coach Cody appeared and waved them back. Right behind him was a tall, skinny guy in street clothes. Black pants, red-striped sport shirt. No cap. Hair on his face. From a distance he looked older than a high school kid.

He dug in at the plate in black dress shoes. He had wide shoulders and a big, open stance, like Billy Budd's. Coach Cody yelled at the pitcher, "See what this batter's got."

Craig Wiebusch, the number 1 starter, turned to grin at the rest of the team as if to say, Meat's gonna beg for mercy when he sees what I got.

The kid waggled his bat like Billy until the pitcher pumped, then he cocked it and froze. He slashed the first pitch down the left field line. DeVon Morris, the third baseman, could only wave at it. Eric lurched after it. Coach Cody clapped twice.

The kid let the second pitch go. It was an inch outside.

Good eye, thought Mike.

He lined the third pitch, a change of pace, over second toward Mike. Ball had speed on it. It was starting to rise, and if Mike hadn't been playing shallow it would have gone over his head. He jumped, caught it. Heavy ball. The kid had power.

He looped the fourth pitch, a curveball, over Andy's head into short right field. Ryan made a nice run, but didn't get close. Kid has great bat control, Mike thought. He can hit to every field. Who is he? This is a tryout. Wonder what position he plays.

Craig looked around, scowling. He hated being hit so easily, shown up in front of the team. Who wouldn't, Mike thought, but it was kind of funny seeing Craig sweat. Craig liked to make other guys sweat.

Craig took his time, as if this were a tight spot in a game, then wound up slowly and fired a fastball at the kid's head. The kid leaned away from it but his heel caught and he fell backward on his butt. Everybody was grinning except the kid and Coach Cody.

The kid got up slowly and dug right back in. Didn't dust his pants or rub his butt, just looked at Craig with no expression. Mike felt a chill. He knew what was going to happen next because he knew what he would try to do.

The kid drilled the next pitch right back at Craig, who barely got his glove up in time to protect his face. The force of the drive spun him around. The ball bounced off his glove as Craig dropped to one knee. Coach Cody was laughing this time. He slapped the kid on the shoulder and steered him off the field.

An assistant coach blew a whistle. They trotted in.

Andy was waiting at first base for Mike and Ryan. "Kid can hit."

"Who is he?" said Mike.

"Illegal. Snuck over the border to play here." Andy side-kicked Ryan and jumped away from the counter-kick. "I keep telling you these guys take jobs away from Americans."

"You nutjob," said Ryan. They box-slapped until Mike pushed them apart.

"C'mon, Coach hates that," said Mike.

"You're a kiss-ass coach's pet, Semak," said Andy. "That was a dumb catch."

"He's just trying to make us look bad," said Ryan.

"Easy to make you look bad," said Andy. He dodged Ryan's soft jab. They all laughed. They'd played together since farm league.

"Where's that kid play?" said Mike.

"Looks like an outfielder," said Andy. "Cody's gonna register him now."

"How do you know?" said Mike.

Andy shrugged. "Happening all over the country. Next

year we'll have to speak *Español* to play."

"*No comprendo,*" said Mike. But he felt a scratch of fear in his gut. What if the kid's a center fielder? He followed his friends to the locker room.

Craig was standing with Todd and Eric. He was still angry. Mike and Ryan avoided catching his eye, but Andy couldn't resist. "It's a brand-new ball game, Craig. Call it . . . *béisbol.*"

Craig cursed him.

"Better learn to say that in Spanish," said Andy. "Or it's *no más.*"

Craig lunged at him but Todd grabbed him and Mike steered Andy away. "What's wrong with you? Got a death wish?" Craig was a team leader, not someone to mess with.

"Truth hurts," said Andy. He looked pleased with himself. He'd rather shoot his mouth off than start on the varsity, Mike thought.

His ankle throbbed. Better ice it right now. But he didn't want anyone seeing him icing it. Can't let anybody think he didn't have two good wheels. He stalled until the coaches had all left, then took a long shower to kill more time. Most kids didn't take showers if they were going home.

By the time he got out, even the trainers and managers were on their way out. He wrapped a towel around his waist and took a cold pack out of the trainers' refrigerator.

He wrapped the pack around his right ankle and stretched out on a trainer's table with a *Sports Illustrated* he found in a pile of magazines. It was the preseason issue with a photo spread on Billy Budd. He'd already studied it at home. He'd been following Billy Budd for eight years, since Billy was twenty and he was nine, each of them a rookie center fielder for the Yankees. Mike was on his first Little League farm team, the Yankees, when Billy was brought up from the minors to the Big Club. They both had rocky starts and then, almost together at midseason, they began pounding the ball. Now Billy was a five-time All-Star with two World Series rings and Mike was on his way to starting in center field for the defending conference champions.

Unless my ankle collapses or this new kid already has the job.

He pushed the thought out of his head. Billy always said you had to stay positive or you'll positively lose. Mike concentrated on the photos of Billy and his latest girlfriend, some model. They looked perfect together.

His cell phone beeped. It was a text message from Coach Cody. It was going to rain tomorrow morning, so he was calling a special Ranger Run. Hope the ankle can take it. No way I can wimp out. Don't think about it now. He stared at a picture of Billy and his girlfriend he had stared at before. They were both modeling underwear, standing in the middle of the vast green lawn outside Billy's Florida mansion. He had a penthouse apartment in Manhattan, too. Billy Budd had it all. And he was nice, friendly, easygoing. Confident. Standing there wearing only boxer briefs, he looked as sure of himself as he did wearing Yankee pinstripes.

"Whose panties are you trying to look through, his or hers?"

He dropped the magazine and jerked up from the table. A black cap hovered above him, the bill pulled down over a girlish face with a sneery grin. The voice was high, with a sharp edge to it.

It took him a moment to realize it *was* a girl. She was tall. She was wearing a varsity track jacket.

He tightened the towel. All he could think of to say was "This is the boys' locker room."

"You think?"

When she pulled off her cap and a landslide of coppery-brown hair fell to her shoulders, he recognized her. Katherine Herold. Last year, at the Varsity Banquet, they had been called to the stage together to receive the Sophomore Athlete Awards. She was on the track team. He'd seen her compete once. She ran the mile as if it were a sprint, flat out. She was the same way in class when she got into an argument, usually something political with Andy. She sounded and looked like the female cops and assistant DAs on the crime shows. He avoided her. She was one of those people who could pull you out of your zone.

She hobbled away.

He felt he had to say something. "What happened?"

"The whirlpool's broken in the women's locker room. As usual."

"Your leg."

"Knee." She didn't look at him.

"I'm almost done," said Mike.

"Take your time," she said. "You don't bother me."

You don't bother *me*. He watched her out of the corner of an eye as she stepped out of flip-flops, stripped down to her T-shirt and running shorts, and unstrapped her knee brace. She turned on the whirlpool machine and climbed onto the ledge. She lowered a leg into the foaming water. She had a nice bod, muscular yet curvy. He looked away when she shot him a glance.

He lay back on the trainer's table. The hum of the machine lulled him. He lost track of time. He drifted to the edge of sleep, then came back. He was hungry. After a while he unwrapped the ice, slipped off the table, and limped back to the lockers.

"You should stay off that ankle," she said.

He didn't turn around. "You think?"

THREE

The house was quiet. The cat met him at the front door and looked up expectantly, ready for a head scratch and dinner. He stepped over her. He didn't like the cat. Too unpredictable in her moods. He'd rather have a dog, but after the last one died they had decided to wait until Dad's second store was opened and running, which was turning out to be harder than Mom and Dad had expected. Nobody was ever around to walk a dog these days. The cat meowed. He changed her water and dropped a scoop of dry pellets into her dish. She dug in and forgot about the head scratch.

Mom had left a note on the refrigerator. As usual, she'd left dinner for him. All he had to do was nuke the chicken and broccoli and dress the salad. Too much work. He made two peanut butter sandwiches. He took them and a container of milk up to his room.

He logged on to the Buddsite. It opened with a montage

of Billy making jumping, diving, sliding catches while John Fogerty sang "Centerfield," the greatest song ever written. That had given Mike the idea of using the opening bars of the song for his own cell phone ring. *Put me in, coach.*

The Yankees were heading back from spring training for opening day at the Stadium. The daily Billyblog was all about how excited Billy was to start the new season. Mike clicked past the links to donate to Billy's charitable foundation for poor kids; to order Billy's book, *IMs to a Young Baller*; to buy T-shirts, jerseys, wristbands, batting gloves, posters, street signs, the wastebasket, the bobble-head doll, the bumper sticker that read WHAT WOULD BILLY BUDD DO? and came with a booklet of twenty-five moral situations and how Billy would deal with them.

Over the years, mostly through birthdays and Christmases, he had gotten everything Billy. He had read the "What Would Billy Budd Do?" booklet a dozen times. It covered everything from injuries to designated driving, but he couldn't remember anything about how to act if some new kid is going to take your position. C'mon, Mike, you're being paranoid. For all you know, Coach was just trying to shake everybody up. He likes to keep us from getting complacent. Andy was talking out of his butt, as usual.

He looked up at the Billy Budd posters on his wall. His favorite was Billy looking straight at him, his mouth slightly open as if he were ready to say something. Every so often he imagined a conversation with Billy, but he didn't feel like having one right now.

He clicked past the Buddline, where you could send Billy a personal question and get a personal answer. He had never sent Billy a question. His questions had always seemed too trivial to bother Billy. And sometimes he thought how bad he would feel if Billy never answered him.

He clicked onto his favorite link, the Billyball instructionals. For the hundredth time he watched Billy position himself to throw home after catching a sacrifice fly.

But he watched it without seeing it and he finished the sandwiches and milk without tasting them. Usually when he felt down, the Buddsite could lift him back up, but it wasn't working today. He felt jostled out of his zone. The new kid. The girl in the locker room. Forget 'em, Mike. As Billy always says, *Keep your eyes on the prize and never quit, young ballers, never quit.*

Center field is the prize. But Mike had a bad feeling that keeping his eyes on it and never quitting wasn't going to be enough.

He had realized how much he loved center field during the last football season. Playing safety was a little like playing center field. The similarities had made him more impatient for the baseball season. In both sports you're a lone rider in your own territory and the game is spread out in front of you. You start moving the moment the action begins. You follow the ball knowing you are the last line of defense. Everything is in your hands. Everyone is depending on you.

But in a football game there are too many variables—enemy jerseys coming to take you out, your own guys getting to the ball carrier first or getting in your way.

Baseball is simpler, purer. Baseball isn't really that much of a team sport. As much as you might be down with the guys and support each other, everybody has his own job and pretty much does it alone. When that little white pill comes off the bat and over the infield, it's all yours. Track it, time its drop, pick it out of a bright, dark, patchy, blue gray sky. Feel it settle into your glove, close your hand around it and then, if there are men on base, maybe someone tagging up to score, turn into position for the long throw home.

He felt better thinking about the fundamentals.

Just before he logged off the Buddsite, a blinking alert popped up. The site was announcing an A Day With Billy contest. He read the rules: The contest was open to any male or female high school varsity baseball or softball player in the metro area. The winner of the best two-minute video essay about what baseball means to him or her would get to spend an entire day with Billy, including a visit to the clubhouse and a meal in the stadium. Mike tried to imagine what that would be like, but his cell phone interrupted the thought, singing, "Put me in, coach." He checked the ID. It was Lori. He felt guilty about letting the call go. She was always so nice, never gave him a hard time. Can't imagine her storming into the boys' locker room. He felt warm remembering Katherine Herold's body perched on the whirlpool ledge.

His eye caught the poster of Billy Budd looking at him accusingly. Billy was big on respect to women. In the IMs book, he wrote: *The mark of a real man is how he treats women, children, and all others weaker than himself.*

You call Katherine Herold weak?

Homework made him feel better. The fundamentals again. Mike's Applied Math teacher, Dr. Ching, had assigned a problem that caught his interest: You are in a boat, on a lake that has a fixed volume of water. You drop your anchor overboard. Does the water level rise or fall? The answer, Dr. Ching said, involves the principle of buoyancy. The problem dated back to Archimedes of Syracuse. Dr. Ching called Archimedes "that ancient dude" and made him sound cool.

Mike enjoyed getting lost in the problem. In math there's always an answer, right or wrong. In baseball games you win or lose. You play or you don't. He liked life simple, like a dog, not complicated, like a cat.

FOUR

Mike loved the Ranger Runs, especially on a damp, chilly morning like this one in late March when the wind drove grit from the track into his cheeks and rattled against his plastic goggles. He'd gotten the idea for the goggles from Billy Budd's book. *Always protect your eyes,* Billy wrote, *because you can't see the ball without them.* The Yankee center fielder would like the Ranger Runs, too. Billy had written that athletes need to keep pushing themselves so their performances are never affected by fatigue. Too many ballplayers give up in the late innings because they are tired or afraid of losing. The tough ones love the challenge and step up their game.

The runs were part of Coach Cody's plan to make them mentally and physically tough for the new season. Coach was running alongside the team, a silver bat in his hand, chanting, "I wanna be a Ridgedale Ranger, I wanna laugh at fear and danger."

Mike led the team with a long, easy stride. The ankle complained softly. He had taped it at home and wore high-top running shoes for extra support. After the first lap the team began stringing out behind him. Hector and Todd, scrappy little middle infielders, were right behind him, followed by the sophomores trying to suck up to Coach.

Ryan pounded along in a pack of other outfielders and pitchers. Andy was cruising in the rear with the catchers and managers. He looked as if he were bird-watching. Didn't he want to start?

Coach Cody came up alongside Mike. "Pick it up, Mighty Mak." Coach rapped the silver bat against his thigh.

Mike felt big and hard, leader of the pack. Billy always led the Yankee runs in spring training and the pregame sprints. Mike cranked up the pace, chanting to blot out the pain beginning to bloom in his ankle. Out of the corner of his eye he saw the tall, skinny kid from yesterday run onto the track behind the stragglers. He was wearing white Nike running shoes now and a black Nike warm-up suit. A white Swoosh cap. Pretty duded up for a Ranger Run, Mike thought. After a few steps the kid pulled out of the inner lane and began moving up on the outside.

Coach hollered, "Let's go, Oscar, see what you got."

Oscar lengthened his stride. He glided past Andy and

was running with Ryan's pack.

Without thinking, Mike ran faster. Coach fell back to Hector and Todd.

It took Oscar less than a lap to pull alongside Mike. They looked at each other. Oscar had a long, dark face with a wispy mustache and a goatee. He did look older than a high school kid. Oscar grinned and raised his eyebrows. A silent drag-race challenge. He put on a burst of speed.

Mike knew better. This was a training run, not a race. A cold morning a few days before the season began was the perfect time to wreck your ankle, pull a hamstring. Be smart and cool, Mike. Let the hotshot go.

Mike took off after him.

Kid's fast, Mike thought, but baseball fast, not Olympic fast. I can take him. *Never quit, young baller.* He zoned into the race, concentrated on bringing his knees up, leaning into the sprint, getting his arms into a rhythmic pump. He heard his teammates cheering him as he pulled up to Oscar.

Coach Cody was standing in the middle of the track near the locker-room entrance, holding up the bat to signal the end of the race.

They finished in a dead heat. Mike was breathing hard. He couldn't tell if Oscar was winded, too. He was smiling at Mike. Friendly-like.

Mike didn't feel like talking to Oscar, but he thought,

What Would Billy Budd Do? He stuck out his hand and said, "Welcome to Ridgedale. I'm Mike Semak."

"Thanks, man." Oscar smiled and pumped his hand. He had an accent. "Oscar Ramirez."

"Where you play, Oscar?"

"Center field."

He said it as if I should have known already, Mike thought.

"See you later." Mike forced a grin and headed for the lockers.

Andy fell into step beside him. "Making nice with the illegal? Gonna give him amnesty?"

"Knock it off," snapped Mike. "He might be on the team."

"Might be?" echoed Andy. "Why do you think he's here?"

Mike walked away, showered and dressed quickly. Coach grabbed his arm on his way out of the locker room.

"I liked the way you welcomed Oscar. That's something a team leader does."

Mike felt a warm flutter. Billy was the Yankee captain. In a few weeks Coach would be talking to the seniors about next year's captain. The seniors made the final selection during a secret ceremony in which the candidate would be blindfolded and run through a gauntlet. Not so secret. It was a tradition, everybody knew about it.

He remembered Oscar.

"Oscar's on the team?"

"Nice kid. Dominican. He can play."

Mike's mouth was so dry, all he could say was "Thenter field?"

"Maybe. Two practices till opening day," said Coach. "We'll see who deserves center field."

FIVE

The ankle buzzed with pain as he walked to homeroom trying not to limp. Anger bubbled up to his chest. He'd waited all his life to start in center field for the varsity and now some new kid shows up to steal it. Immigrant. Probably illegal.

Slow down, you're starting to sound like Andy. You don't know anything about this kid. And who says he can take center field away from you?

"Got a minute for the planet?"

At first he thought it was one of Andy's riffs. He liked to mock environmental activists. Mike was in no mood for Andy's crap today. He said, "Bite the planet."

As he said it, he saw the clipboard with a pile of papers and Zack Berger's tangle of curly black hair.

"It's your planet, too, Mike, and unless we . . ."

The anger was in his chest. "I'm late for class."

"It's late for Earth," said Zack. He had a deep, older voice that Mike had heard for years in political debates and election speeches, and in announcements for the Cyber Club. Mike could usually shut it out, but today it scratched his nerves.

"You're in my way."

"This is really important," said Zack. His eyes were boring into Mike. He had the clipboard inches from Mike's face. He was almost as tall as Mike, but he was narrow, a skinny neck and no shoulders. You could tell he never played ball. As usual, he had his dorky black bag slung across his chest.

"Important to you." Hot and bitter, the anger stung his throat.

"We all . . ."

"Move it."

Zack didn't move. ". . . have to step up . . ."

Mike pushed the clipboard aside, scattering the petition and a pile of colored papers on the hallway floor. Some of the papers were green. Mike thought of new grass.

Zack held his ground. ". . . even dumb jocks who think the planet exists just for them." There was spittle in the corners of his mouth.

Mike hit him.

Mike didn't think he hit him hard. More of a shove than

a punch, a thump to the middle of Zack's chest with the heel of his hand. The kind of hit they threw in the showers all the time. Nobody ever went down.

Zack went down. He flopped like he was trying to con a referee into calling a foul, thought Mike. And then he banged his head on the hallway floor. The sheets of paper Mike had knocked out of his hand were spread around him.

There was a silent moment. Kids in the hallway froze. Then teachers rushed over to Zack.

Coach Cody materialized out of a wall.

"What's going on?" He grabbed Mike's left triceps, digging in hard, holding him in place until one of the teachers helped Zack to his feet and nodded to Cody. Then Cody steered Mike to his office. He had forgotten how short the coach was. His shaved bowling-ball head only came up to Mike's chin. And how wide. The man was thick, all muscle. He was built like a Hummer.

He didn't let go until they were inside his office, door closed. He pushed Mike into a wooden chair. He perched on a corner of his desk. His friendly position. He sighed. He didn't seem that angry.

"Bad blood between you two?"

Mike shrugged.

Coach Cody leaned forward. His face was inches away.

"Talk to me." He smelled of soap and cologne. He had just taken a shower, too.

The anger had drained out of Mike. He felt empty. Weak. "No excuses."

"No kidding. Tell me a story."

"We had words," said Mike. "It got physical."

"You got physical. What did he say?"

"Nothing much." How could he say that the kid was winding up to give him a lecture and when he called him a dumb jock I lost it? Dumb, maybe. But not much of jock if I'm not going to start.

"A skinny computer nerd says something and you knock him down. What's wrong with you?"

Mike shook his head. I don't know what's wrong with me, he thought. A half hour ago in the wet cold I felt great. Now I feel like crying. He clenched his teeth to keep his stony expression from cracking. I'm not going to cry. You can expel me. I don't care.

Send me to jail. I'll play center field in jail.

"You're a prospect, Semak, not a suspect. A coachable kid. A starter this season. A team leader. Something's going on here. What is it?"

Without the anger, Mike felt small and weak. What is going on?

"Jocks are the heart of this school, Mike. Focused,

disciplined, strong. Role models. The other kids look up to you."

Nobody needs to look up to me, thought Mike. Just let me play. He looked down at his tan work boots. He wore them during the season so spikes would feel lighter on his feet. Make him faster. Billy did that.

"You react to someone like Zack Berger, you make him a victim. People feel sorry for him, maybe even listen to him. Jocks are bigger than that. You tracking me?"

Mike nodded.

"Can't hear you."

"Yes, Coach."

After a while Coach Cody said, "Sit tight." He marched out of his office. The two-way radio in his back pocket crackled something about an ambulance.

SIX

Mike stared out the window. Gray, rainy day. Fits my mood.

Phones rang. Period bells clanged.

He stared at the pictures on Coach Cody's wall.

Cody getting a plaque from the mayor and the chief of police. Cody showing a senator around the school. Cody with last season's baseball team after winning the conference title. Mike was in that picture.

Cody posing in a camouflage uniform with an automatic rifle. Must be from when he was an Army Ranger. There was a sign in the background with Arabic letters. He didn't like to talk about the places he'd been and what he'd done there.

Tough guy. That's why he'd been hired as dean of discipline five years ago. There had been gang violence and drug dealing in nearby New Jersey towns. The school board was afraid it would spread to Ridgedale. Mike was in middle school when Cody arrived but he heard about him from his older brother, Scotty. Cody was kind of a mystery man, which made him seem even tougher. No one knew if he was married, or even where he lived. There were rumors he had worked in law enforcement, even Homeland Security. He scared people.

Cody instituted zero tolerance policies. He searched kids, busted into lockers, shut down the school newspaper when it complained. Some parents threatened a lawsuit but gave up the day Cody pulled a pistol out of a kid's backpack. The kid claimed he had never seen it before, that the gun had been planted. He was expelled.

Cody was promoted to vice principal, and to celebrate he took over the baseball team. That was two years ago. His first season was Ridgedale's first winning season in ten years. He could pretty much do what he wanted without checking with anyone else. He'd driven the players hard and some quit, but he gave the team pride in itself with tougher practices, stricter dress codes, one-strike-you're-out for smoking, drinking, fighting, don't even dream about drugs.

He even changed the school teams' nickname from Ridgerunners to Rangers. He made athletes feel superior to anyone who wasn't one of them. He liked hard-nosed play-ers who would run through a wall.

Last year he'd been at the JV game when Mike slid so hard headfirst into the opposing catcher that he dropped the ball. Mike scored the winning run. Cody came into the locker room afterward and on the spot promoted Mike to the varsity. He was only a sophomore. Cody made a little speech about how you don't really know what's inside yourself until the chips are down and you have to either step up or wimp out. Mike Semak stepped up.

He got into a few games and even started one, in center field, when the regular, a senior, got hurt. Mom and Dad showed up for that game. Mike got two hits and made a running catch. It was the proudest day of his life.

It seemed so long ago.

Maybe I should have told Coach Cody what happened, he thought. What *did* happen? Stupid. Zack Berger's been on everybody's case all year about global warming and health care and immigration and AIDS in Africa, and some local program to teach disabled kids and old people how to use computers to make the world better. He'd been in my face before and I just walked away. Why did I lose it today?

My ankle?

The Dominican kid?

I'm supposed to keep my cool. It's what ballers are trained to do. You don't let yourself get distracted, thrown off your game. Billy Budd's advice was to take a deep breath and count to three. Or repeat the name of your favorite ballplayer three times. Billy's favorite when he was a kid was Kirby Puckett, the Hall of Fame center fielder for the Minnesota Twins. When he felt himself getting angry or losing concentration, Billy would say *KirbyPuckettKirbyPuckettKirbyPuckett*.

Mike said, *BillyBuddBillyBuddBillyBudd*.

Why didn't he do that today?

You never give the opposition the satisfaction that they got to you. Don't get mad, get even. A wide receiver shoves you, just make sure you disrupt his route. Pitcher brushes you back, get a hit. Or drill one back at him, like Oscar Ramirez did.

A new center fielder takes a couple nice swings and you go batshit and shove a nerd. Get yourself thrown off the team, just what Oscar wants. You're supposed to step up to the challenge. That's what real jocks do.

Mike remembered that first year when he and Billy were struggling. There was talk that the Yankees were going to trade for a veteran center fielder and send Billy back down to the minors. Billy didn't lose it. He stepped up his game. He nailed his position. You've got to do the same thing.

If Cody lets me.

What can I say to him?

And to Dad? Mike felt a stab of dread. Dad was going to be pissed big-time. He's got a lot on his plate these days and he doesn't need me messing up. Scotty in graduate school and Tiffany alone in the city with her little kid and especially the new store about to open. Dad and Mom talk about money all the time. Loans and mortgages and lines of credit drying up. I know he's counting on me to win a Division I athletic scholarship to pay for college. They had money for Scotty's music lessons and college, and for Tiffany's therapy and special schools. But things are tough now.

How could I screw up like this? I'm supposed to be the steady kid in the family, the dependable one.

Mike wasn't counting bells so he didn't know how much time passed before the door opened and Cody marched in—with Dad a step behind, breathing fire.

"How brain-dead can you get?" Dad yelled.

"Hello to you, too," said Mike.

With his left hand, Dad grabbed the front of Mike's shirt and yanked him out of the chair. He was roaring, "This is not acceptable," when Cody pulled Dad away.

"Easy, Mr. Semak. We'll handle this."

"Whatever you decide, Mr. Cody, you have my full support. Demerits, detention . . ."

"Could be suspension," said Cody.

"Well." Dad made one of his palms up gestures. "Boys will be . . ."

"Not on my watch."

"Of course," said Dad, dropping his hands, backing up. Over Cody's shoulder, Dad winked at Mike. He's telling me to be cool, Mike thought, he's got a plan. "What do you want me to do?"

"Take him home, Mr. Semak. I appreciate your cooperation. But give us a chance to sort this out." Just the way Cody said it, Mike had the feeling the coach was impressed by Dad's hard-nosed, take-charge attitude.

As usual Dad has a scheme, thought Mike. He felt safer, but smaller.

SEVEN

Out in the hall Zack Berger was being comforted by the principal and his mother. Mike had seen Zack's mom around the school, volunteering in the library. Just like a nerd, thought Mike, gets all that attention for a little shove. A jock would have picked himself up and shaken it off.

Dad marched right up to them, tugging Mike along by his shirtsleeve.

"I can't tell you how sorry I am about this," said Dad, his voice booming in the hallway, "unacceptable behavior."

They all took a step back. The principal, Dr. Howard, said, "After a complete investigation, we will be in contact." Mike thought she looked at Dad as if he were an unfriendly dog, off the leash.

Zack's mother said, "This may be a police matter."

Dr. Howard said, "That's your decision, of course, but . . ."

"She's right," said Dad. "If schools can't keep boys from

fighting, maybe the cops can."

The principal's nostrils flared. She didn't want cops in her school. Zack's mom blinked hard. Dad had called her bluff, thought Mike. She didn't want her son mixed up with the cops, either. Zack was probably a stoner. Dad has moves. The tricky old salesman.

Dad put his hand out. "I'm Scott Semak."

"Denise Berger." She gave his hand a quick shake. "I've passed your store in town."

"We're opening another one at the Valley Mall. Stop in." He gave her a card. "I'm not sure who's at fault here, Ms. Berger, but I can tell you how disappointed I am that Michael was involved. It's a difficult age but that's no excuse." He grabbed Mike's triceps harder than Coach Cody had. "Let's go. You've got some serious explaining to do, young man."

He dragged Mike away. Mike felt even smaller, weaker. He hated the look on Zack Berger's face; the nerd feels sorry for me.

Dad pulled him through the hall toward the front door. Mike caught a glimpse of Coach Cody, arms crossed over his big chest, a smirk on his face. What was he thinking—now that I'm rid of Semak, I can put Ramirez in center field?

Outside, Dad walked Mike through the rain and shoved him into the front passenger seat of his green Prius, the car he used when he was hustling clients who cared about the environment. He usually drove a Lexus SUV. Once they were out of the entrance parking circle, he said, "I think we're okay. Kid's not hurt. I made 'em feel bad for you. No charges, no lawsuit."

The old phony wants me to give him a standing O, thought Mike. He stared out the windshield through beads of icy rain.

"So what happened?"

Can't talk to him, thought Mike. "Drop me off here. I'm in the varsity lot."

"Varsity lot." Dad shook his head. "You know the first thing Coach Cody said to me? Responsibility goes with the varsity letter. You can't act like a dumb jock."

Mike glanced at him, but Dad was turning into the varsity lot, no expression on his face. Dad is not subtle, thought Mike. If he knew what Zack had called me he would have slapped me around with it, not just dropped it in.

Dad was looking around. "I don't see the Jeep."

"I rode my bike."

"In this weather?"

He'd been through this before and didn't feel like going through it again. Billy Budd rode his bike through sandstorms and ice storms, whatever the weather threw at you in Centerburg, Colorado. That's why he never got tired now, why his legs were steel.

Dad pulled up at Mike's specialized hybrid locked to a

light pole. "I'll call Cody later. Might have to lay some tile in the locker room."

Mike opened the door and stepped out. He met Dad's eyes as he closed the door. The old bull artist looked sad. Trying to make me feel guilty, thought Mike. I am guilty. How stupid can I get?

Mike unhooked the batting helmet from his backpack. He put it on and fastened the special strap to keep it snug. The helmet was like the one Billy wore as a kid. Protected your head while it got you used to wearing a batting helmet. Until the Yankees made him stop, Billy rode his bike in spring training and sometimes even to the Stadium.

Mike slipped his backpack on and unlocked the bike. The Prius hadn't moved. Dad was still watching him. Thought I might go back and hit Zack again?

What's wrong with me? I am a dumb jock, he thought. Dad always waits to make sure I'm okay before he drives off. Does it for all his kids. Always has. He has our backs, best he can.

Mike waved and pushed off. Once he was out of the lot and on the road, pedaling hard into the chill wind, he felt a rush of endorphins, the natural chemical that kicks in during exercise. Billy said they were the only drug you needed.

EIGHT

The cat was not happy to see him. Her eyes narrowed as if to say, You came home early to mess with me. He leaned down to give her a head scratch and she took a swipe at his hand with a claw. Near miss.

He pulled an ice pack out of the freezer and wrapped it around his ankle. Some of the chicken Mom had made for him yesterday was in the fridge. The only orange juice he could find had pulp. He took milk instead and went upstairs.

His cell was going off but he didn't open it. Everyone would want to know what happened. He didn't want to think about it. Stay focused. Work out, do some homework, use the day productively. He remembered one time when Billy Budd's best friend on the team, Dwayne Higgins, was suspended for five games for charging the mound after getting plunked, Billy had him stay at his house and use his personal gym. He came back in better shape and had his best season.

Try not to think about Billy. He avoided looking at the poster. Forget about center field. Forget about baseball. Coach Cody is going to kick me off the team. He has a zero tolerance policy for almost everything. He liked playing for Coach. All you had to do was follow his rules and do your best and you were okay. Ryan felt the same way about the coach. Andy didn't like Cody, said he was devious, that he messed with your mind. But Andy had a problem with authority. Didn't like to take orders. The way Andy was going, he might not have to listen to Coach much longer. Me, either. Mike felt like crying. But jocks don't cry.

He couldn't concentrate on homework and there was no classic ball game on ESPN. He felt as though he were sinking underwater, losing breath, moving in slow motion. He searched for an old *CSI*. He didn't watch a lot of TV besides sports, but he liked these shows, where the bad guys get nailed after an hour of methodical, logical science. He finally settled for an ancient *Law & Order* with a sexy, sharp-faced assistant DA who looked like Katherine Herold. He remembered her in the locker room and felt a splash of heat, then began drifting away.

Footsteps on the stairs woke him. Mom ran into his room and leaned over the bed to hug him. "Are you okay?"

"I'm fine."

She sat on the bed. "What did that jerk say to you?"

"Nothing."

"He must have said something to provoke you."

He felt like he was lying when he said, "I don't want to talk about it," because he knew she would take that answer to mean she was right.

"You know we're behind you."

"Thanks," he said. He believed her. They had always trusted and supported him. He hated to disappoint them.

She hugged him again. He felt like a child. "This is such a stressful time for all of us. And you've always been such a good kid." She paused and her eyes filled up. He knew she was thinking about Tiffany. "I'm so sorry I wasn't at the school for you."

"Dad was there—it . . ."

"I was in the city buying carpeting. I'd never have agreed with Mr. Cody. It couldn't have been all your fault."

"Agreed with Cody about what?"

"I cut a deal." Dad was in the doorway, looking smug. "I know these law and order types."

"What kind of deal?" said Mike.

"A little community service," said Dad. "And a meeting with the school shrink."

"Shrink?" said Mom. "You didn't tell me that. I don't

think that's a good thing to have on your record."

"It's district policy," said Dad, waving it away. "One session. Doesn't appear on your record if nothing else happens. I checked that out."

"What kind of community service?" said Mike.

"Help out the computer geeks. Clean up, whatever." Dad chuckled. "Delete their porn."

"Great." Zack was in charge of the Cyber Club. Now I'll have to listen to him lecture me, too.

"Think about what Cody could have done," said Dad. "Not to mention a lawsuit."

"But Mike didn't hurt that boy."

"Get some doctor to claim back injury. Happens all the time. Cody said he'll make sure there would be no—"

"Mike was provoked," said Mom. "Maybe it was self-defense."

"You got to see this skinny nerd," said Dad.

"Coach say anything about the team?" said Mike.

Dad shook his head. "Sounds like he's counting on you to play. Long as you do your couple of Saturdays for the computer club."

"This Saturday?" said Mom. "I was hoping Mike could come with me into the city. Sophia hasn't seen her uncle Mike since Christmas."

"Be grateful we dodged the bullet," said Dad. "All we

need with the new store."

"Scott, that's not the only thing . . ."

"Right now it is."

She sighed. "I'll put lunch out."

When she left the room, Dad said, "Lucky you hit the right kid. Cody doesn't like him."

"He said that?"

Dad grinned. "Cody and I understand each other. Kid's a troublemaker. He pushed your button. Understandable. Let's go eat." He grabbed Mike's arm and pulled him off the bed. "Got sandwiches from the deli."

Downstairs, Mom and Dad began talking about the new store as usual. Mike thought he should be glad the discussion about him was over, but he felt dissatisfied. He realized he wanted a little more attention, maybe even some questions he wouldn't answer.

Don't be a baby, Mike. You're still on the team. Pretty soon there'll be green grass on the field.

NINE

When he rode up Saturday morning, Zack was waiting behind the school, checking his watch. It was only a few minutes past eight o'clock. So the nerd's going to be like that, thought Mike. Be a long day.

Mike took his time locking his bike to a pole alongside a battered white van with CYBER EXPRESS and an email address on the doors. He'd seen the van around but never paid much attention. It was never in the lots where he parked.

"Wasn't sure you'd make it," said Zack. He didn't seem all that thrilled that Mike had made it.

"Nothing better to do," said Mike.

"You could have iced your head," said a girl, opening the van door and climbing out. It was Katherine. She looked different. The landslide of coppery hair was in a ponytail pulled tight and high. It looked good. He was surprised he noticed. Lori complained that he never noticed how she looked, that he didn't really look at her at all.

Mike said, "Is listening to you part of my community service?"

Zack glared but Katherine grinned. She likes getting under my skin, Mike thought. Coach Cody had made it clear yesterday there'd be a report from Zack, and it had better be good if Mike wanted to stay on the team. Dad had given him a little lecture, too; sometimes you have to play along so you can play.

"You here to work or mouth off?" snapped Zack.

Mike took a breath. *BillyBuddBillyBuddBillyBudd*. "What do you want me to do?"

"Kat and I need to take equipment to the senior center in Bergen Falls and set up," said Zack. "Okay?"

Kat was a good name for her, Mike thought. He shrugged. "Whatever."

Zack and Kat exchanged glances and Zack rolled his eyes. Mike wondered what that meant. Probably just ranking on me. Try to get me to shove him again, get thrown off the team and out of school. No way. *BillyBuddBillyBuddBillyBudd*.

Zack had a key to one of the back doors the school custodians used. It led to the Cyber Club's basement room, which had two sets of locks on the door. Mike had never been inside the room. No windows. There were long tables against each of the four dingy green walls. Old computers sat in nests of wires. There was a round table in the middle of the room with cameras and printers.

It took them almost half an hour to unhook four desk-tops and their accessories and pack them into padded boxes. Zack and Kat did most of the work. She was wearing loose warm-up pants but he could see the outline of her knee brace. She limped slightly, but she carried heavier weights than Zack. They really didn't need me, Mike thought. He carried the boxes out to the van; as much as he didn't want to be here, some part of him wanted to do his share.

He rode in the back of the van to Bergen Falls, to an apartment building near the railroad tracks. He'd passed the three-story heap of yellow brick hundreds of times on the way to ball games but never really seen it.

He carried the boxes into the basement of the build-ing and helped Zack and Kat unpack. They began reas-sembling the desktops. They worked quickly and precisely. Kat pointed to stacks of wooden folding chairs against one chipped green wall. "You might want to set them up, maybe twenty, facing the computers."

Where do you learn to talk like that, he thought. You *might want to* set them up. And then I *might not*. And you *might want* to stick them . . .

Suck it up, hoss.

He nodded. He really didn't mind having something physical to do.

About nine thirty old people began coming in. Kat said

to him, "You might want to stand by the door if anyone needs help."

"I just might want to do that," he said. He turned before he saw her expression. That was stupid, he thought. But what do you expect from a dumb jock?

Gray heads bobbed past, a zombie parade, he thought, a lot of them shuffling behind canes and walkers, but a surprising number bouncing in on running shoes. He watched a shapeless old woman lurch forward gripping the silver pipes of her walker. She wore a lot of makeup caked in her wrinkles. Dyed red hair stuck out from under her New York Yankees cap, which she wore backward. One of those crone characters out of a sitcom. Somebody's nutty grandma.

A couple of kids from school showed up to help the old people send emails and pictures. One of them was a skinny Goth kid who looked familiar. Mike caught them looking at him and whispering. He glared back. They looked away.

Mike's mind drifted. Monday and Tuesday were going to be big days, the last two practices before Wednesday's opening game, the last two chances to show Coach he was a better center fielder than Oscar Ramirez. How good is Ramirez? If he fields as well as he hits, pretty damn good. Got to focus, get into the right mood. The way Billy would. Billy had all the right instincts, he always knew what to do, on the field and off. Having all the tools, even the tactical smarts, isn't enough. You need to be zoned. Billy is always zoned. Billy is perfect.

It's too hard to model yourself on perfect. In Youth Group, Pastor Dan would say that you can't really be like Jesus but you can take inspiration from Him. Billy might have been in a basement like this—he did a lot of charity work. But he'd be here because he wanted to be here, not because he shoved some skinny nerd.

There was a low hum of talk in the room, interrupted every so often by laughter or a shout. The zombies seemed to have come alive. The Ridgedale kids were having a good time, too. Some part of Mike wanted to be part of this, not just alone in a corner. He plugged himself into his iPod and listened to a playlist Lori had made for him as a six-month anniversary present. Too many love songs. He hadn't gotten her anything because he hadn't even remembered they had an anniversary. They'd drifted into being a couple early in the football season. She and her twin sister, Tori, were twirlers on the cheerleading squad. Really good. It was rare for sophomores to do as many routines as they did. Ryan had hit on them first and then dragged Mike along as his wingman to a concert the twins had scored tickets to. They had all gotten along well. Mike was never sure how they decided who got which twin. It took a while to tell them apart. Lori's giggle helped at first, then their personalities emerged. Lori was sweet. Tori was tough. Lori liked to read books and talk about them. Tori was addicted to gossip—school and celebrity. Ryan seemed to like being bossed around by Tori. Mike liked how Lori let him stay in his zone. Respected his space.

He tried to think about Lori, but there wasn't all that much more to think about. He realized he wasn't looking forward to seeing her tonight. He heard Kat urging an old man to try moving his mouse a little more firmly. It was the first time he hadn't heard a sharp edge to her voice. She was smiling as she leaned over to guide his hand. Her breasts brushed the back of his head. The old man didn't notice. Mike felt warm. He looked away.

And then Zack was thanking them for coming. Next week, he said, they would join internet groups. There was applause. Mike was surprised to realize it was already past one P.M.

While the old people took their time leaving, he helped Zack and Kat unhook the computers and pack them up. He carried the boxes out to the white van.

The old lady in the backward Yankees cap was one of the last to leave. He held the door for her. She said, "You don't look like a computer brainiac to me."

"I'm the dumb jock bodyguard," he said.

She threw back her head and laughed. She repeated the

line to a few people before she shuffled out.

Back at school, after they unloaded and rehooked the computers, Kat said, "Wonder why we have to do all this? The school can spend a hundred thousand dollars on sports equipment, a new weight room, indoor and outdoor batting cages, you believe that? But they can't come up with more money for secondhand laptops for outreach programs that benefit the entire community."

Zack said, "He can read it all on RidgedaleReform dot org."

"Like he can read," said Kat. "Or cares."

Zack turned to Mike. "You coming next week?"

The question puzzled him. "Coach Cody said you wanted me for three weeks."

Kat and Zack exchanged glances again.

"Fine," said Zack. "Same time and place." It had started raining. "You want a ride home? There's room for the bike in the van."

"I'm okay." It came out more sharply than he had intended.

"He can get wet," said Kat. "He's a dumb jock body-guard."

TEN

"I know Zack Berger," said Lori. "He's very intense."

Ryan made a slurping sound. "And tastes so good."

Lori's twin, Tori, hit Ryan with a French fry. "He comes to more cheerleading shows than you."

"To hand out propaganda," said Andy.

"So at least he considers them important," said Lori.

"To dump on America," said Andy. "Tell me why some geek who thinks he knows everything can say anything he wants and get away with it and if I say certain things I'm a bigot."

"We love you but you're a bigot," said Lori.

"If Mike had slugged me, he'd of gotten a medal," said Andy.

"I'd give him one for that," said Ryan.

"Mike shouldn't have hit him," said Tori.

"He must have been provoked," said Lori. She sounds like Mom.

"Now shut up," said Ryan. "It's on." He tapped the mute

button on the remote and a cage fighter who looked like a gorilla started explaining the rear naked choke like an English teacher might explain Melville.

"Are these guys actors?" said Lori without moving her head from Mike's shoulder. They were on the big leather couch. She was playing with Mike's hair. He was enjoying it and annoyed at the same time. She always had her hands on him. He didn't feel into it right now.

"Mixed martial arts is the latest weapon of mass distraction," said Andy. He lowered his voice and continued talking to Lori, who nodded, wide-eyed. He loves to hear himself, thought Mike, and she thinks he's so smart. I don't even feel jealous.

He didn't feel like being with them or watching the fights. If his sore ankle wasn't propped on the arm of the couch, wrapped in an ice pack, he would get up and leave. Then what? He didn't feel like being with himself either.

And where would he go? They were in his house, in one of the best media rooms in town, an eighty-four-inch pull-down screen in front of them, a high-definition video projector on the ceiling, decks of DVD, CD, and iPod players, speakers angled off the ceiling and walls. Dad had set up the basement rec room as a place to entertain politicians, clients, and suppliers when he opened the first store in better days, but he didn't use it much now.

There was a popcorn machine and a refrigerator stocked with soda, white wine, and beer. The liquor cabinet was locked but Mike knew where Dad hid the key. Could use a belt of Captain Morgan right now, but he didn't dare open the good booze. Ryan and Andy knew how to soak it up.

Lori whispered, "Whatcha thinkin'?" She was always trying to get closer. Inside his mind.

He shook his head, thinking he'd be fine with every-one leaving right now. Andy and the twins wanted to meet up with some other kids in Nearmont, but Ryan wanted to watch some of the cage matches first and Mike said he needed to rest his leg. He really didn't, but just thinking about a crowded party filled with new people had darkened his mood. He wanted to walk into a room as the center fielder of the Ridgedale Rangers, not just another jock scrambling for a starting spot on the varsity.

I need sunlight, he thought, a new season. Put me in, Coach. Center field.

Tori said, "So what did they make you do?"

"Move stuff around," said Mike. "They went to a senior center."

"The Crumblies," said Lori. When everybody looked at her, she said, "That's what they call old people in this book

I'm reading about the future where they make everybody pretty and dumb at sixteen."

"Sounds like the present to me," said Andy.

Lori giggled, a tinkly sound that once had seemed cute to Mike.

"So what did you do there?" said Tori.

"They showed them how to send pictures to their grand-kids," said Mike.

"It's a cover to spread left-wing propaganda," said Andy.

"I'd rather spread left-wingers," said Ryan.

"That's demented." Tori poured popcorn on his lap.

Ryan laughed. "Now you gotta eat it, no hands."

I wish they would just disappear, thought Mike.

"Zack give you a hard time?" said Andy.

"Why would he do that?" said Lori. "Mike was helping out."

"Geeks are into payback," said Andy. "Weak bullies are the worst."

"Tigerbitch there?" asked Tori.

"Who?" said Mike. But somehow he knew. Felt excited.

"Katherine Herold," said Tori. "The guys on the track team call her Tigerbitch."

"Why?" said Mike.

"Mood swings," said Tori. "She can be nice one day, nasty the next. Same day sometimes."

"Sounds like our cat," said Mike. He wanted to hear more.

"Maybe she's like bipolar," said Lori. "I read this . . ."

"She just hates men," said Andy.

"She just hates you," said Ryan.

"I thought she was Zack's girlfriend," said Mike. Why am I fishing for information? Zack didn't have girlfriends.

"You sound interested," said Lori in her cutesy voice. Must be jealous, Mike thought.

"She's too complicated for Mike," said Andy.

Lori's face got soft and hurt while Tori's tightened up. They were identical twins, short, dark-haired with pretty faces and pert butts and boobs, but they didn't even look like sisters when Lori got that wounded look and Tori leaped to defend her.

"What does that mean, complicated?" snapped Tori.

"She's political, she's smart," said Andy. "Although misguided in her beliefs. A terrific athlete. You know, she's also a really good filmmaker?"

Lori looked like she was going to cry.

"I bet it was Tigerbitch's idea to make Mike work for them," said Ryan. "To keep him away from twirlers."

Lori relaxed and laughed but Tori kept glaring at Andy.

"It was Cody's idea," said Andy. "Everything he does is

designed to keep us off balance and retain his totalitarian control of the school."

"*The Chocolate War*," said Lori. "I read that last year."

"If it's in a novel," said Andy, sneering, "it must be true."

"You should read more," said Lori. "It helps you understand relationships."

"Andy doesn't need to understand relationships because he doesn't have any," said Ryan.

Mike was trying to think of a way to get the conversation back to Kat when Tori said, "Can we go now?"

"The twin has spoken," said Ryan, rising.

Lori untangled herself from Mike and helped Tori straighten up the room.

I'll bail out by complaining about my ankle, thought Mike, and then I'll feel angry at myself for lying. But I'll explode if I have to be with them much longer.

He could predict what would happen next. Andy, Ryan, and Tori would head off to Nearmont. Lori would stay but she wouldn't make a fuss when he said he was in pain and wanted to get to sleep. She'd be disappointed, which would make him feel bad, but she'd say she was in the middle of a good book to make him feel better. She'd wait to be sure her sister and the guys were gone before she went home. She wouldn't want them to think she was getting kicked out, too.

He knew he'd be glad to be alone, but he'd be lonely,

too. He could take a Vicodin for the pain in his ankle or a shot of Captain Morgan for the pain in his head. Never both, a deadly combination. How about neither? Suck it up.

What's wrong with me? Why do I treat Lori like this? Because I can? Never get away with being like this with Tigerbitch.

ELEVEN

Coach Cody pulled him out of his last class of the day, a study hall for jocks, and walked him toward the front offices. "Talk to me. Saturday. Zack Berger."

"We took computers to the senior center in Bergen Falls, brought them back."

"What were they computing?"

"I think they were teaching them to send emails and pictures."

"Think? What were you doing?"

"I wasn't paying much attention." Thinking about center field. He wondered if he should ask about that.

"Got to stay in the now, wherever you are," said Cody. He put a hand on Mike's shoulder. "A lot of intangibles go into how I set my roster, you know what I mean?"

"No," said Mike. He looked Coach in the eye, but broke contact first.

"There are a lot of ways to help the team," said Coach.

"Stay awake next week. I want to know exactly what they're up to. Go get ready for practice."

By the time Mike dressed and ran out to the field, Coach Cody and his assistant coaches were running positioning drills. They would be repeating them all season but never as intensely as now. Coach always said that fatigue lost games and fundamentals won them. Maybe he'd read Billy's book, too. The basic drills taught you what to do and how to do it while the Ranger Runs made sure you had the stamina in the late innings to concentrate and execute.

Today they were drilling outfielder positions on balls hit to infielders. It was routine on most plays, backing up the infielder in front of you. Follow the ball. It would become more complicated soon, Mike knew, depending on the score of the game, how many outs, how many runners on base. He loved that part of baseball, the thinking and remembering part, the math and science of it, as much as the pure athletics of running, catching, throwing, and hitting. He twisted his fist in the oiled pocket of his glove.

Oscar was all over center field, moving at the *ping* of the ball against Coach Cody's silver bat. Oscar was quick enough to back up Eric in left and Ryan in right, and he charged in so fast on balls that scooted through the hole that he often had the chance to throw out the runner at first. His arm was a live whip. Oscar was always in the right spot.

Mike wondered if he had attended one of those baseball academies in the Dominican Republic he had read about in *Sports Illustrated*. They were operated by major league clubs. They were set up like real schools except kids didn't study much besides baseball.

After a while Coach Cody waved Oscar in and sent Mike out to center. As they passed near second base, Oscar gave Mike a wink. Hector Ortiz saw the wink and said something in Spanish. Hector and Oscar laughed.

Mike pushed down his anger and focused on Cody at home plate. "Sharp now. One out, runner at third." He signaled Oscar to run at third.

One out, thought Mike, sacrifice fly, tag-up situation. Depending on the batter and the score, he might play deep or shallow. Just be ready. Easy drill. Done this a hundred times.

Soft fly to center. Ryan and Eric ran over to back him up. Mike moved in, set himself, felt the ball settle into his glove. Oscar was running. Andy had moved over from first to set up a line from center to home, to guide the throw. He'd cut it off if Oscar went back to third, otherwise get out of the way.

Should be an easy out.

Hector ran to his right to cover second in case Mike dropped the ball. That was right. But Hector was yelling at Andy, what the hell was he saying? For an instant Mike lost concentration. He paused in his throw as Andy got out of the way. The catcher was crouched at the plate, waiting. Mike pegged home.

Oscar was sliding under the tag. He bounced up, dusting off his pants and laughing. Hector was laughing, too.

Had he distracted Mike to make him look bad? Come on, that's really paranoid. You let yourself get distracted. But Andy was yelling at Hector and Cody was shouting, "Stay alert, Mike." Just what he needed to hear. Now say it in Spanish for the illegal.

It didn't get better. Oscar ran out to replace Eric in left and beat Mike to a soft fly in short left center. Could have been either fielder's ball, but the center fielder, the stronger fielder, usually takes those. Then Coach Cody waved Mike to left and Oscar back to center. Give me a chance to get settled into my position. It is my position, right?

"Men on first and third, no outs, we're leading by one run in the seventh." Coach lofted a high fly deep into left center. There was plenty of time for Mike to get under it and set himself for the throw to nail the runner at the plate and prevent a tie game.

It was the left-fielder's ball, Mike thought, my ball, as he took a few steps toward center. But if Eric was in left and I was in center, I'd probably poach, take it because I was a better fielder with a better arm. Billy Budd would have taken it if his best friend Dwayne Higgins was in left. Mike sensed Oscar moving toward him, but that was okay, he was supposed to back up the left fielder.

Just to be sure, Mike called, "I got it."

Oscar yelled, "I got it."

"Mine," yelled Mike.

Oscar ran into him. They both went down. The ball dropped and they both bounced up, cursing and swinging at each other. Todd and DeVon Morris, the third baseman, were there before they could dig in their spikes and connect with real punches. They snarled but they separated.

Coach Cody was laughing. "Got to work on that."

Work on what, Mike thought. Me in left? The thought of it made his stomach hurt. He hated left field, right field, too, the cramped space, the foul line, all those tricky angles, none of the wide-open purity of center.

They ended practice with wind sprints. Mike made sure he beat Oscar, but he wasn't sure Oscar was going all out.

Back in the locker room Andy said, "It's happening every-where."

"What?" said Ryan.

"If the Chico was under the ball and called for it and

Mike ran into him, it would be considered a bias crime. Zack Berger would be out demonstrating."

"Not so loud," said Mike.

"You gotta do something."

"Like?" Mike looked around. Oscar was in the showers.

"Check his immigration papers," said Andy. "Check his age, he could be too old for high school ball. He might have a pro contract already. He might not even live in the district. Check his address, he might be ineligible."

"Get a life." When Andy shrugged, Mike said, "What did Hector yell at you?"

"Said to get out of the way, you had a great arm."

Somehow that didn't make him feel better, and he scowled at Hector when the little second baseman came over tugging Oscar. "He got something to say, Mike."

"Sorry, man," said Oscar. He looked sorry, eyes down. "Back home I take everything."

You're not in your home now, you're in mine, Mike thought, but he nodded and mumbled, "Forget it."

After they walked away, Ryan said, "Don't sweat it, bro, you'll start in center. You can't have an illegal in center field, it just isn't right. Joe D. and Mickey would roll over in their graves. Even Billy Budd would be out demonstrating."

PART TWO

"You can't win the pennant on opening day,
but you can start trying."

—*IMs to a Young Baller* by Billy Budd

TWELVE

The sun came out for the opening game.

The school day had lasted forever but passed in a blur. Sunlight hammered the dusty classroom windows, blotting out words on the page, drowning teachers' voices, making Mike jittery. Move it, he urged the clocks on the walls. He winced remembering the last time he had said, "Move it." To Zack.

Dr. Ching asked if anyone had the answer to the dropped anchor problem. Does the water level rise or fall? No one raised a hand. Mike knew the answer but he couldn't get his mind focused. He was thinking about center field. Am I starting today?

"Buoyancy," prompted Dr. Ching.

One of the math brainiacs finally raised a hand, but she needed help from Dr. Ching to make her answer clear to the class.

Anything that displaces water is buoyed upward by the

weight of the water displaced. The boat and everything in the boat must be displacing an equal weight in water, otherwise the boat would sink. While the anchor is in the boat, the anchor displaces an anchor's weight in water.

But when the anchor is dropped, it sinks, displacing an anchor's volume of water. Since the anchor is denser than water, an anchor's volume of water is less than an anchor's weight of water. So there is less water being displaced, and the overall level of the lake drops slightly.

The water lowers, not rises, when the anchor is dropped.

I could have done that, thought Mike. Did I choke? Will I choke in center field? Will I get the chance to choke in center field?

Lori stopped him in the hall. "You okay?"

"Why?"

"You're, like, sleepwalking?"

Luckily he was called on only once, in Contemporary Social Issues. Ms. Marsot asked him to make comparisons between immigration today and a hundred years ago, but before he could even say "Huh?" Andy shouted out, "It's mostly illegal now," and Kat said, "But it's still supply and demand." Ms. Marsot leaned back with a smile and let them take over the class.

He usually tuned out the Andy-Kat Show and drifted into his own thoughts, but today he kept watching Kat.

Those deeply set dark eyes under thick eyebrows made her seem even more intense. He remembered her body while she sat on the edge of the whirlpool machine, soaking her leg, her breasts against the old man's head at the senior center. She kept those muscular curves pretty well covered in class. Today she was wearing a loose sweatshirt and jeans baggy enough to fit over the brace. You'd never know how packed she was.

He pushed his thoughts back to center field.

Coach Cody waited until they were finished with batting practice and warm-ups and had turned the field over to the visiting team before he made his pregame locker-room speech. It was usually a short review of the scouting report and a few things to remember during the game, but this afternoon he was revved up. He strutted to the front of the locker room after the assistant coaches herded everyone together.

Chest out, muscles bulging through his Ridgedale uniform, cap pushed back on his shaven head, Coach Cody looked like he could take anyone on the team in a cage fight. The rumor was he had racked up kills in Panama, Kuwait, and Somalia as a Ranger. He rocked heel to toe a couple of times, scanning the team until everyone was in their places and quiet. Seniors were sitting on the floor up front. Mike, Andy, Ryan, and the other juniors were right behind them.

"We are about to embark on a mission," said Coach Cody, "in which we will seize the state championship." He tamped down the whistles and cheers with his thick hand. "A three-month mission by a band of brothers, elite athletes with the training, the skill, the heart, and the smarts to make their will prevail.

"Just like the Army Rangers who fight and die to protect our country, you are focused, dedicated young gentlemen who know how to shut out everything that doesn't contribute to the success of our mission."

"Mission?" whispered Andy. "It's baseball."

Mike elbowed him quiet. He wondered if Coach had heard. He was looking at them when he said, "Not everyone in this school is on our side. There are teachers who don't like jocks and girls who want to drag you down and the pukes who hate you because they can't ever measure up.

"You need to stay together, listen to your coaches, support your teammates, follow the rules, execute with pride, and play your guts out. No one is shooting at you Rangers, but just because we call it a game doesn't mean that winning isn't real, isn't important. Just because we call it a game doesn't mean that your willingness to work hard, to sacrifice, to put the team ahead of yourself, isn't the best thing you can do."

"What crap," whispered Andy. Mike ignored him.

Coach put his hands on his hips and grinned. "The envelope please." He took a blue sheet of paper from a manager as if he were at the Academy Awards. He began to read, pretending to be surprised. "Leading off and playing second base for the champion Ridgedale Rangers, it's . . . Hector Ortiz."

"Like he doesn't know his opening-day lineup," said Andy.

Mike's mouth was too dry to tell him to shut up. He managed, "Sssss."

"Batting second, at shortstop, Captain Todd Ganz." The team whistled and clapped.

"Bastard's playing with our heads," said Andy.

Coach might have heard but he didn't react. "Batting third, in center field . . . Mike Semak."

It wasn't until Ryan yelled, "Yo, Mak," that his mind processed the information. He was starting. In center field.

"Batting cleanup, in left field, Oscar Ramirez."

There were groans from the seniors. The regular left fielder, Eric Nola, was a popular guy.

Dimly Mike heard Ryan Gates in right and DeVon Morris at third and Mark Rapp at first base. The sophomore had beat out Andy. Jimmy Russo was catching and batting eighth. Craig Wiebusch was pitching.

"That's today's lineup, gentlemen, and it will change as

you change." Mike thought Coach was looking at him. "I will choose the best player for each position. Every inning of every game is a test of the best." He clapped his hands. "RIDGEDALE!"

Everybody grabbed for the nearest two teammates and roared, "RANGERS!"

The subs led the way out of the locker room, then the starters. Mike didn't have time to say anything to Andy. He jogged out to center field between Oscar and Ryan. Both of them were nodding and smiling. Once they were in position, they began throwing a ball around.

The stands weren't crowded, but they weren't empty either, a good turnout for a baseball game in a football and basketball school. He looked for Mom and Dad. Maybe they'd come later. The band was playing and the cheerleaders were doing cartwheels. They only came out for opening day and the postseason tournament.

Tori and Lori ran out. They looked hot in their blue and gold tights as they danced through their devil stick routine, juggling a baton with two control sticks, sometimes passing batons between them. They were good—they would be competing in a national championship tournament in a couple weeks. Lori threw him a quick smile and a head wave without losing her rhythm.

He swept the stands one more time. Mom and Dad said

they'd try to make it, at least one of them, but it would be tough. The floor was being laid in the new store, and in a flooring store it had to be perfect. He didn't see them.

He spotted Kat on the sidelines aiming a video cam up at the principal, Dr. Howard, who was high in the grandstand waving a Ridgedale pennant in a group of teachers. He watched Kat limp over to the stands and sit next to Zack, who had a pile of leaflets on his lap. Kat raised her camera. It was too far to tell if she was aiming at him or at the scoreboard behind him.

THIRTEEN

Craig Wiebusch was sharp in the top of the first. Three up and three down, a strikeout and two infield grounders.

From the dugout Mike began studying the Southwood pitcher, a tall, gangly junior Mike remembered from football, a backup quarterback. He was fast and wild, which kept most batters from digging in close to the plate. Scouting reports said he depended on the burner, but could fool you with an inconsistently nasty slider and a good changeup. Mike tried to see if he gave his pitches away. Some pitchers hunched over a little more before throwing a curve, straightened up before a fastball.

Coach Cody was coaching at third, flashing hand signals that didn't mean anything. Ranger psych tactics, he called them. He said it distracted the opposition, frustrated them into making bad decisions. He said it was worth a run a game. Hector, leading off, didn't need any instructions. His job was to get on any way he could.

Hector's specialty was driving pitchers crazy, stepping in and out of the box, fouling off pitches. He worked the pitcher for a walk, then kept taking leads off first and scrambling back while Todd waited for a pitch he could bunt. Everyone knew he was going to bunt, but if the pitcher didn't throw a strike, Todd would walk, too. Finally he threw one low that would have clipped the outside corner if Todd hadn't reached over and tapped a beauty down the first base line. The catcher threw him out but Hector was dancing on second base when Mike came to bat.

Coach Cody touched the bill of his cap, pulled his left earlobe, and rubbed the letters on his chest. Ignore everything until he shouted, "Let's go, Mike," and clapped twice. The signal after that was the one. Coach leaned over with his hands on his knees. Hit away. No kidding. This early in the game it was all about piling up some runs, giving Craig a lead.

The pitcher hadn't tipped off his pitches so Mike set himself for a fastball. Always easier to adjust for a curve than try to catch up to heat. The first pitch was high and inside enough to make Mike lean back. Hard to tell if that was on purpose. Mike fouled off the second pitch, a curve. Now he'll come in with heat, Mike thought, try to overpower me. Coach Cody was rubbing his left elbow. Meant nothing.

"Curve," said Oscar from the on-deck circle.

Like he would know, thought Mike. His first game in this conference, hasn't even had his first at bat and he's an expert. He felt that little bubble of anger in his gut, the same one he had felt before he shoved Zack. The thought was distracting. Gotta get rid of it. He stepped out of the batter's box, took a deep breath, thought *BillyBuddBillyBuddBillyBudd*, and stepped back in before the umpire could warn him about delaying the game. He set himself for the fastball. If it was a strike he'd try to drive it into right field, score Hector. There was a big hole between the first and second basemen.

The pitcher grooved it, down the middle. Thanks, pal. Mike took it late and opened up to hammer it into right. But the ball slowed, broke inside, and dropped. Frantically he still tried to make contact. He punched a hopper past the pitcher. The shortstop scooped it up, bluffed Hector back to second, and fired the ball to first. Mike was out by two steps.

He avoided looking at Oscar as he trotted back to the dugout, head down.

Ryan slapped his back. "Wicked curve, Mak." He was on his way to the on-deck circle.

Mike shook his head. I blew it, he thought. And Oscar knows it.

They watched Oscar take his stance. Hector took a lead,

yapping at the pitcher. The second baseman stayed close to
the bag. Coach Cody was yelling, "Two out, two out."

Oscar was cool at the plate. He let two fastballs go by,
both of them outside. The umpire called the second one a
strike. Coach Cody yelled something, took off his cap and
slapped his shaven skull, gleaming in the afternoon sun.
That meant, You're a numbskull, ump. Coach Cody was a
master of sly little insults but he knew how far he could go
without getting warned or thrown out of the game. He said
you had to keep pressure on the umps so they didn't think
you were a wimp who would roll over for them. Ranger
psych. Worth a run a game.

A curve broke inside and Oscar checked his swing. The
ump called that one a strike, too. Mike figured that meant,
Shut up, Coach, don't try to make me look bad.

Oscar's expression never changed. He was in the hole now,
one ball, two strikes. The pitcher is mixing his pitches pretty
well, thought Mike. See if Oscar can figure them out.

Another curve that broke close to Oscar's hands. He
fouled it off.

The pitcher took his time now. He glared at Oscar. No
question now, he was going to challenge him. Heat. He
reared back and blazed one in.

Oscar hardly seemed to move his body, just flicking his
wrists. Contact sounded more like *pong* than the *ping*. The

ball flew on a straight line between first and second and landed deep in right field. Hector scored easily and Oscar was on second before the relay throw came in.

Coach Cody was clapping and cheering as Ryan got up to bat. He nailed the first pitch and sent a long drive to deep left. Oscar was rounding third as the left fielder pulled it down. Inning over. But the Rangers led, 1–0.

In center field Mike avoided looking at Oscar, even though as captain of the outfield he should be checking the positions of the other outfielders. He thought, Just try to stay inside yourself today. Too many distracting thoughts.

Craig was on fire all afternoon. He rarely fell behind in the count, and even when he did, he challenged them to hit his fastball or chase his changeup. Southwood didn't get a man into scoring position until the sixth, and then Oscar made a fine running catch along the left-field foul line, whirled, and threw a bullet to DeVon at third when the runner at second tagged up. He was out by two steps to end the inning.

Craig waited on the mound until Oscar trotted past and bumped fists with him. Craig had forgiven Oscar for making him look bad the other day. At least for now, thought Mike. Good for the team even if I'm not having much of a day. That's the way Billy Budd would think. Mike bobbled a routine fly in right center, although he held on to it. His ankle ached and he was a step behind a long drive to left-center that hit the fence. Oscar was backing him up and fired in to Todd to keep the batter at second.

It was worse at bat. Mike was lunging at the ball, never making solid contact. He was overeager and knew it and couldn't do anything about it. He hit into a double play and popped up to the catcher.

But the one-run lead held into the seventh when Oscar blasted a homer with Todd on base. The final score was 3–0.

Oscar was the man in the noisy Ridgedale locker room. He looked happy but humble, slapping palms, bumping fists. Mike thought it would be easier to dislike him if he were cocky instead of just confident. Why should I dislike him? Why shouldn't he be confident? He can play.

Craig followed Oscar around, holding up his boom box. Chief Loki was screaming, *"We own da season."* Oscar looked embarrassed.

Mike dressed and got out as quick as he could. Didn't have a chance to ask Oscar how he knew it was going to be a curve. Baseball instincts or had he spotted the pitcher's give-away motion? Maybe I don't want to know, Mike thought.

FOURTEEN

Coach Cody and Oscar didn't show up for Thursday's practice. According to Ryan, who heard it from Tori who volunteered in the school office, they were going to see an immigration lawyer.

"Get him an instant green card," said Andy. "Special dispensation."

"For what?" said Ryan. They were standing at the new batting cage, waiting to hit.

"He has a skill in demand," said Andy. "He can get us to state."

"A little early for that," said Mike. "Just one game."

"Andy's right, he can play," said Ryan.

"What I'm saying is that the system is corrupt," said Andy. "I bet Oscar's twenty if he's a day, probably spent a few years in the rice and beans league back home. He's a pro, ineligible to play high school ball. Bet he has an agent.

You notice the brand-new Nike gear he wears?"

"Coach Cody wouldn't allow that," said Mike.

"Wake up and smell the burritos," said Andy. "Cody brought him in to make us winners."

It was Mike's turn to hit, and he was glad. Got to concentrate. Get my swing back. Nice and easy, just make contact.

One of the assistants, Coach Sherman, just a few years out of college, was pitching batting practice, grooving fastballs. After Mike slapped the first two pitches back to the screen in front of him, Sherman yelled, "You're hitting on top of the ball, Mike. Watch the bat make contact."

He finally managed a solid hit, a rope to left center, on his last swing. As he ran to first, Coach Sherman yelled, "Attaboy, Mike," which made him feel worse. Getting praise for something he usually did all the time was a warning signal.

You losing it, Mike?

He didn't see Coach Cody or Oscar in school on Friday and Tori didn't have any more information. She and Lori were sitting with him and Ryan at one of the varsity tables. Andy had stopped to talk to some girls on the debate team. Girls who liked jocks usually didn't go for him.

"You think Oscar could be twenty?" Ryan asked.

"Who said that?" said Lori.

"Andy."

Tori snorted. "Like he knows."

"I thought you can't play if you're over nineteen," said Lori. "Don't they have our birth dates on file?"

"Those files are in Coach Cody's office," said Tori.

"So Coach would know," said Mike. "Can we talk about something else?"

"*Billy Budd*?" said Lori. She was trying to be nice, Mike thought. "The book was summer reading last year. It was so sad when Billy died at the end."

"Another parable about good and evil," said Andy, arriving with his tray. "Evil always wins in Melville. Check *Moby-Dick*."

"Billy Budd's such a great name for a baseball hero," said Lori.

She's trying too hard, thought Mike. She's starting to annoy me. He'd make some excuse not to see her tonight. Saturday night the twins were having a party at their house, parents away, no way to avoid that without breaking up, which was too much trouble.

Andy was shoveling French fries into his mouth as Kat strolled past, her video cam in one hand. She stopped and said, sharply, "The point you don't seem to get is that undocumented workers only take jobs Americans don't want."

Andy said, "They work so cheap Americans can't compete for those jobs."

Kat curled a lip at his fries and cheeseburger. "No wonder your mind's clogged."

Ryan said, "You never outgrow your need for trans fats and toxic chems."

Everybody laughed except Kat, who gave Ryan a nasty look. She was in a bad mood, thought Mike.

Andy said, "You love your government control so much, how about regulating organic farming. It's all agribusiness now anyway."

She frowned and nodded. "You might be right. Even a stopped clock is right twice a day." As she walked away, Mike noticed that she had a swing to her butt. Maybe it's her rehabbed knee.

Ryan said, "Tigerbitch wants to jump your bones, Andy."

"That'll be the day." Andy made a snorting noise, but Mike thought he looked interested. He felt a twinge of jealousy. Kat had never even looked at him.

He was alternately sorry and glad Friday's game was rained out. He wanted to get back out there, redeem himself, but he had a nagging fear that something was wrong, that he was in a slump that could cost him center field. Coach Sherman reminded them that next Saturday morning, a week from tomorrow, they would be attending a hitting clinic at the Meadowlands. Team bus will be leaving at eight A.M. High school teams from all over the metro area will be instructed by major league players and coaches. Maybe some Yankees. Mike wondered if Billy Budd would be there.

He lost himself in the Buddsite that night. He watched an hour of the sweetest swing in baseball, short and whippy. Shoulders relaxed, eyes tracking the ball from the pitcher's hand to the surface of the bat. Billy never stopped to admire his hit, just peeled off for first base, running hard unless it was out of the park. If it was a homer, he would slow to a jog, head down, never hotdogging, never smacking on the pitcher, just acting lucky to be here. Not acting, Mike thought. Billy was for real. Lucky Billy.

A chat room message popped up from EmoBaller, a high school outfielder from Connecticut. *How opening game?* Mike wrote back, *We won I sucked. In a slump.* EmoBaller wrote *Hit the Buddline.* Catchergrrl, a Long Island softball player wrote, *Like Billy knows about slumps?* They exchanged LOLs on that but Mike wasn't in the mood to chat, especially when Catchergrrl and EmoBaller started trashing Billy's girlfriend, the model. They agreed she looked cold and plastic. Mike wasn't interested in criticizing Billy's taste in women.

After a while he logged onto the Buddline. A picture of Billy popped up. He was leaning back in the dugout, elbows hooked on the back of the bench, smiling. "How can I help you, young baller?" he said.

A space opened up and the words *Please type your question for Billy here.*

Mike wrote: *I'm in a slump at the plate and in the field. What should I do?*

It took a while to bring himself to click on the HIT IT bar. My first question ever. Am I that desperate?

He hit it.

The Billy poster on his wall nodded. *You did the right thing, young baller.*

Probably be a day or two at least before there would be any answer, he thought. If ever. Next game is Tuesday. Hope I hear something before then.

He wandered downstairs. Friday night was a big night at the old store. Mom and Dad would be there, one or both of them rushing back and forth to the new store as problems cropped up. Their opening day was coming soon. He knew they would like him to get involved in the business. That pressure was only going to get worse, he thought. Scotty was serious about graduate school and a career in music, no way he was going to let them drag him into the business. And Tiffany had always had enough trouble taking care of herself. With a kid now . . .

The cell was beeping. Texts from Lori and Ryan. He ignored them. See ya tomorrow, leave me alone.

He thought about Vicodin and Captain Morgan, maybe just a beer, but ended up with milk and a chunk of the chocolate cake Mom had left with his dinner. Tomorrow was an early call. In some weird way he was looking forward to the Cyber Club. Kat.

He climbed back upstairs, careful on the ankle, barely avoiding the cat crouched on a step hoping to trip him. He was tired and would have settled for a *CSI* he had only seen two or three times, even an *NCIS*, which was too jokey, but the Billyblog was blinking and beeping with an alert. MESSAGE FROM BILLY!

And there it was. *I don't believe in slumps, Mike, and neither should you. We all have good days and bad days. The trouble is, when you get down on yourself during a bad day, it doesn't go away. Start thinking about the good days you've had, days when the baseball looked big as a beach ball coming out of the pitcher's hand and you were all over it. Think about days when you wanted every ball hit to you and you sucked them up like a vacuum cleaner. Visualize those days and they will come back. Good luck, Billy.*

He felt short of breath. Sounded just like Billy, positive and constructive. He could imagine Billy's voice, deep and friendly, giving him the advice. He imagined Billy sitting in front of his locker, typing on a laptop balanced on his knees. That was silly. Billy's game was rained out, too—he wouldn't even be at the stadium. At home, maybe, with the model.

FIFTEEN

Zack and Kat were already inside the basement room, unhooking computers, when he walked in. She was wearing a varsity track warm-up suit in the blue and gold Ridgedale colors, but the letters spelling out Rangers across the front seemed to have been torn off. Weird, thought Mike.

"Didn't think you'd show," said Zack. He looked sorry to see Mike.

"We had a bet," said Kat. She looked glad. "I won."

"Why'd you bet on me?"

He was surprised to see her blush. The question had knocked her back. What happened to cool Kat? It took the Tigerbitch a moment to get her claws out. "I figured you'd do anything not to play baseball, the way you're hitting."

Somehow the dig pleased him. He'd gotten to her and she needed to snap back.

"Let's get to work," said Zack.

* * *

When the shapeless old woman in the backward Yankees cap lurched into the senior center behind her walker, she yelled, "Where's my dumb jock bodyguard?"

An old man whispered to Mike, "She's been talking about you all week."

"I heard that," she said. "I like big bad boys. C'mere."

Kat was trying not to laugh. Mike walked over. The old lady looked like one of the mythical beasts they'd read about in Freshman English. Harpies? Gargoyles?

"What's your name, hunk?"

"Mike Semak."

"What's your sport?"

"Baseball."

Her eyes opened wide, a surprisingly sweet blue in that pleated, painted face. "Let me guess. You're an outfielder."

"Center field."

"My favorite position," she said. "Okay, here's the deal-break question. Who was the greatest center fielder of all time?"

She was so over the top that Mike felt relaxed with her. He rubbed his chin and pretended to be thinking deeply. "Well, my dad would say Mickey Mantle and I think you would say Willie Mays but I say Billy Budd."

Her shriek stunned the room. Trembling old people

froze. "I'm taking this boy home with me. I love him!" She threw one big soft arm around Mike's neck and hugged him. "Brains and brawn, you can't beat it."

She let go and lurched off to the coffee and bagel table. Mike felt a smile crack his face. He liked the way everyone was looking at him. He searched for Kat. She was pretending to be busy with her camera, but she was laughing.

"Real character," said the skinny Goth kid who had looked familiar last week. "She used to be an actress." He stuck out his hand. "I'm Nick."

Mike suddenly recognized Nick Brodsky, a senior. He was much thinner and more Gothed out than he'd been during football season. Eyebrow rings, which the coaches would never have allowed, black eyeliner, spiky black dyed hair, and a web tattoo crawling up his neck. He'd been a good wide receiver, fast and smart; he could read the defense and beat the corners. Mike liked to practice against him. It lifted his game. He was sorry when Nick quit the team. Something about drugs, maybe even dealing. Tori had heard he was working off his sentence buying cigarettes in local stores so the cops could bust them for selling to underage customers. How had he not recognized Nick last time? Pay attention, Coach had said. Stay in the now.

"Didn't get a chance to talk last week," said Nick. "I wasn't dissing you."

"No offense."

"No defense." They laughed. It was an old football joke. Mike was glad there was another jock in the room. "I heard about you and Zack. He can be intense."

"I should've stayed cool."

"Then you wouldn't get to be here." Nick's whole body rippled when he laughed.

Kat was walking backward, shooting video. When she passed them, she snapped, "Bond on your own time, boys, we got to set up." Still in a bad mood.

Nick whispered, "Tigerbitch!"

"She's okay." Why'd I say that, thought Mike.

Nick rolled his eyes. "You kidding?"

Mike finished setting up the chairs and got himself a bagel and orange juice. At least they had the regular stuff here, no pulp. I should remind Mom, but she's so busy these days.

He watched the old folks. It looked like high school, pushy people grabbing seats at the computers, shy ones hanging back, gossipers in the corners. The old Yankees lady was reapplying her makeup. He wondered if she was really interested in computers or just lonely. Why am I thinking about her?

After a while, when one of the computers was free, he amazed himself by walking over to her and saying, "I'm no brainiac, but I can help you get online and surf around."

"Now that would be grand," she said. She extended a

hand. "I'm Regina Marie. What's your name again?"

"Mike."

"An excellent name, simple and to the point."

He helped her settle into the chair in front of a desktop. "Is there somebody you'd like to send an email to?"

"All dead, honey. What do you look at when you, uh, surf?"

"Billy Budd's got a website. Would you like to look at that?"

"Not exactly Willie Mays, but what the hoo." She laughed deep in her throat.

Mike logged onto the website and showed Regina Marie how to click onto links. She laughed when Billy appeared and said, "How can I help you, young baller?"

"You know, I was one once," she said.

"A young baller?"

"Actually, that meant something else in my time, but never mind." She rolled her eyes. "You know, I played short center field for the *Kismet* team in the Broadway Show League in Central Park. You ever hear of the musical *Kismet?*" When Mike shook his head, she said, "I was a harem girl. Almost sixty years ago." She clicked the mouse. Billy invited her to check out his blog. She read it chuckling. "That girlfriend of his. What do you think?"

"Okay so long as he keeps his eye on the ball."

She laughed until she started choking. He patted her back, not too hard. She liked that. He tensed up when he noticed that Kat was shooting them with her video cam, but Kat noticed his discomfort and turned the camera away.

The blinking alert popped up for the A Day With Billy contest.

"You should enter that," said Regina Marie.

"You need to do a video." Mike shrugged. "What would I say?"

"Talk about center field. I was on the *Today* show once and Dave Garroway, bet you never heard of him, asked me to close my eyes and describe what it was like to sing and dance on a Broadway stage. Close your eyes."

This is too weird, he thought, but he closed his eyes.

"Not so scrunchy," she said. "Better. Okay, Mike, so what's it like being in center field?"

He visualized himself alone on a carpet of dark green late-summer grass, under a ceiling of blue sky, gliding toward a falling fly ball. He heard himself talking. "Center field's part of the spine of the team. Catcher, pitcher, shortstop, center fielder. Can't win without a strong spine."

When he stopped and opened his eyes, the old lady said, "Is it hard to play?"

"It's not as hard to play as shortstop or catcher, all the things they have to keep in their minds. Center field's simpler that way but if you mess up it's going to be an extra-base hit. You have to zone in on the ball, track it right into your glove, and then know what to do with it.

"People always say Billy Budd's a natural, like he was born a center fielder, like it's all muscle memory and hand-eye coordination, but I know how much work went into it, thinking all the time, all the possible situations, how many on, how many outs, which base would you throw to. It's like a math problem, there's a right answer and a wrong one, but you have to figure it out. You can't fake it."

Why am I blabbing like this? He stopped again.

"What else do you like, Mike? Close your eyes."

He closed his eyes again. He was back in center field, the green grass under his feet, the blue sky above.

"It's like being on top of the world. Seeing everything spread out in front of you. Coming at you. It's all up to you, you're the last chance and you've got all this green room to run down the ball. It's open and clean, no foul lines or crazy angles or base runners, just you and the ball."

His eyes snapped open. He had drawn a crowd. He saw Zack with his mouth open, silent for once, Nick grinning and nodding. Kat had the camera aimed at him. People stood behind her. They clapped. His face felt hot.

"Pure poetry," said Regina Marie. "You're ready for prime time."

"Sorry, I . . ." He shook his head. "I'll show you how

to move around the Buddsite."

It seemed like only a few minutes later that one of the old men was thanking the Cyber Club. As he reached over to log out, Regina Marie hugged him. It felt like being smothered by one of Mom's down comforters. It didn't feel too bad.

On the way out Nick high-fived him. "Awesome."

Back at school he thought they unloaded and rehooked more slowly than last week, as if they weren't in such a hurry to split up.

Zack said, "That was a good connection with that woman, Mike." It sounded like praise from an English teacher. "It's the first step. The personal comes before the political."

"It was just nice," said Kat. She sounded impatient. "Does everything have to be political?"

"Everything *is* political," said Zack, "whether you know it or not."

"Whether *I* know it or not?" said Kat. Tigerbitch had her claws out.

"It's an expression," said Zack.

"Mike was reaching out," said Kat. "He wasn't sucking up to her for votes or for some ulterior purpose."

"His motivation is irrelevant," said Zack.

"Of course it's relevant why you do things," she said.

"Only results count," said Zack. He still sounded like

a teacher. "Once you make a human connection you can talk about anything. For example, why genocide is linked to globalization."

"Lighten up, guys," said Mike. "I just got carried away."

"Mike has a history of getting carried away," said Kat. She looked at him. "But it sounded real to me." The sharpness was gone. She smiled.

His chest throbbed. Without thinking about it, he said, "If you're free tonight, Tori and Lori Burkis are throwing a party."

"The Twirling Twins?" said Zack. He rolled his eyes.

"Mike and Lori are an item," said Kat. Mike thought there was an edge in her voice. How would she know, or care?

"Andy will be there," said Mike, mimicking her tone.

"Andy Baughman, the right-wing kook?" said Zack.

"In that case . . ." said Kat.

SIXTEEN

"Why'd you invite her?" Lori's little pout was the closest she ever got to expressing anger at him. Show some annoyance, Mike thought. It would be more real than the pout, which was getting less cute every time he saw it.

"For Andy," he said. "I think they've got a thing going."

Tori made a face. "They hate each other."

"There's a real thin line between love and hate," said Ryan from the couch. "And I've snorted it." He and Mike had come early to help the twins get organized, but Ryan was watching the Yankees game.

Mike was excited about seeing Kat tonight. He hoped Tori was right, that Kat and Andy hated each other.

Lori dragged him down to the basement and pointed out the cartons of soft drinks. He wasn't to bring up the beer and wine until after Amanda, the oldest of the four Burkis sisters, left for her own party. She was a Rutgers cheerleader and super straight. Their parents were at a gymnastics meet in Philadelphia with their youngest sister.

By the time Mike had lugged up the soda boxes, Amanda was gone. He rapped Ryan on the top of his head. "Open up. Police."

"Your bud's up." On the TV screen Billy was at the plate, standing straight, legs wide, bat back and waggling. His laser eyes were on the pitcher. "Oscar copied that stance. Never stops moving the bat but still whips it around."

"Why do you spend so much time watching Oscar instead of working on your own pathetic swing?" Mike tried to make it sound like a needle, but it came out a whiney question.

"I have a man crush," said Ryan. He grabbed his crotch. "Mo's have more fun." He lowered his voice. "The twins can't figure out why you invited Berger and Tigerbitch."

Billy drove a pitch deep into left, a homer or a long out, but he didn't pause to watch it. He put his head down and raced to first as if he were trying to beat out a grounder. He was rounding the bag when the left fielder pulled it down at the wall. He stopped, turned, and jogged off the field without expression. Icy control, thought Mike. That's what I have to work on.

"C'mon, Ry," said Mike, pulling on Ryan's arm. "We got to bring up the booze."

Ryan grumbled but stood up to throw a long soft jab that Mike easily slipped. He led Ryan downstairs, glad to have dodged answering the question. I don't know why I invited them. Actually, I do.

The party started slowly, mostly girls at first, pretending to admire each other's clothes while they glanced around for the boys. He pretended to be watching them while he glanced around for Zack and Kat.

The guys started showing up, mostly junior football and baseball players he knew. Lots of fist and shoulder bumps. They stood around trying to out-cool the hot sophomore girls swirling around them. It was hard to tell who was hunting and who was being hunted. After a while Mike gave up on Zack and Kat coming and let himself flow into the party. He was aroused by the looks he was getting and the seemingly accidental body brushes. He let the music wash over him, mostly Lil Potz and Pug Brown being horn-dogs and Kallie D. singing about doing a girl and a guy the same night and not seeing the difference. He didn't much like the music but after a couple of beers it didn't bother him.

He started talking to a tall majorette who reminded him of Kat. She kept leaning closer and closer to hear him even though he wasn't whispering. They were almost chest to chest when Tori made one of her periodic sweeps through the room and steered him away, claiming she needed his help. She pinched him hard before she parked him with Lori and Ryan. Sometimes he thought Tori was overprotective of Lori and sometimes he thought Tori wouldn't mind switching. Tori has too many sharp angles for me, he thought. Yeah, so why *did* you invite Kat? Not thinking straight?

By now the hard booze had appeared. A few kids were trading shots. A girl was already booting in a downstairs bathroom.

Ryan poked him and pointed. Andy had two girls cornered in the living room. They looked bored.

"Somebody's got to tell him chicks dig the long ball," said Ryan, "not political lectures."

Mike nodded, but thought, Except maybe Kat. He wondered what she was doing tonight. Was she doing it with Zack? Why was she with *him*? Girl as cool as her with such a dork made no sense. She could be with anyone. Maybe she's really into politics. Why do you care so much? What's got into you?

A few kids disappeared upstairs. He smelled pot and moved away. He didn't want to get busted for something he didn't even enjoy.

He was bored but he couldn't leave and he didn't feel like getting hammered so he wandered away for a bathroom pit stop he didn't need and then strolled out toward the front living room. Andy was standing alone, looking lost. Mike realized they still hadn't talked about Andy losing first base to Mark Rapp. He was waiting for Andy to say something. Was Andy holding it all in? Maybe he didn't really care.

"Wassup, Andy?" When he didn't react, Mike thought of something Zack had said to provoke Andy. "Nobody interested in the link between genocide and globalization?"

Andy did a comic double take. "What are you smoking?"

"You think I'm just a dumb jock, huh?"

"Among other attributes." Andy pretended to defend himself against a punch, then pointed over Mike's shoulder. "Am I dreaming?"

Zack and Kat had just walked in. They stopped at the glass cases of trophies and plaques, the pictures on the walls of the four Burkis girls in action.

Mike hurried over. "Hey. Didn't think you'd come."

"Hope you didn't bet against me," said Kat. She sounded bubbly, on top of the world. A different Kat. They both laughed.

She looked great, a frilly white blouse and tight black pants molded to her long, lean legs. No knee brace. She was wearing bright red lipstick, almost dazzling against her pale skin. Her coppery hair was twisted into a giant braid that fell over one broad shoulder. When she leaned over to read one of the plaques, he saw the Chinese characters tattooed on her lower back.

"Victoria and Loriane," she read. "I didn't realize Tori and Lori were nicknames."

"Typical liberal disdain for common people," said Andy. He and Kat beamed at each other. Maybe they did have a thing.

"What are you guys drinking?" said Mike. If I play host, he thought, maybe they'll stay awhile. At least her.

"Beer," said Kat, and Zack nodded.

"Right back." He rushed to the kitchen, grabbed a couple of cold ones, and rushed back. He felt charged.

A few kids had gathered and Zack was already making a speech. "A shrine to futility," he said, dismissing the glass trophy case with a wave. "What could be more useless than twirling?"

"Maybe drinking beer and talking about twirling?" Mike handed them bottles. He liked the way Kat laughed, her dark eyes flashing at him. "What do you think, Kat?" Had he ever said her name out loud before? It filled his mouth.

"I think Lori and Tori are serious, gifted athletes," she said, "who deserve at least as much respect as the tubs of lard on the offensive line. Just because they're women . . ."

". . . doesn't mean we have a right to devalue their athleticism," said Zack, waving a glass as Tori and Lori walked over. "Although wouldn't it be better for them to actually compete in a sport instead of cheering guys on?"

Tori said, "This is such bullshit. My sister and I bust our butts for ourselves, our family, and our school, not so some phony intellectuals can make believe they are on a Sunday talk show."

"Way to go!" said Lori. She hugged Tori.

Zack said, "You're right, Lori." He was sounding like the politician looking for petition signatures. "I'd like to apologize."

Tori snorted and said, "Don't patronize us." She stamped away.

"They're not exactly identical twins," said Mike. He tried to swallow his laughter when Lori shot him an annoyed look. Good for you, finally. She stamped away after Tori.

Kat said, "You can't bring Zack anywhere." She didn't seem embarrassed.

"So send him home," said Andy. "We need to discuss the global warming scam."

"That why it was getting so hot in here?" said Mike. He liked the look Kat threw over her shoulder at him. Hot eyes.

Zack said, "Gotta book. A geek party. Thanks for inviting us."

Mike followed them out the door. "Jock parties always get a little rowdy."

Zack nodded as if it was no problem. "Time off for good

behavior next Saturday. We're going into the city for a conference."

"Might be interesting," said Kat. She smiled at him. His
stomach jumped.

"Wouldn't be interesting for him," said Zack sharply.

"Wish I could," said Mike. "Baseball team clinic. A Major
League hitting instructor is coming."

"Better not miss that," said Kat. It didn't sound sarcastic,
he thought, just sort of playful. Am I hearing what I want
to hear?

He was sorry to see them go.

Everybody was waiting for him. Tori said, "Now I understand why you slugged him, Mike."

Lori said to Andy, "I think Tigerbitch really does like
you." Mike thought it was for his benefit.

Andy ran a freckled hand through his red hair. "What's
not to like?"

"Your personality, your face, and your body," said Ryan,
grabbing him around the neck.

Mike had promised to help the twins clean up, which was
okay, but somehow the trip upstairs with Lori afterward
seemed like a chore. Ryan whispered, "And now, folks,
for some real twirling." Mike punched him but his heart
wasn't in it. Climbing the stairs with Lori tucked under

his arm, he imagined himself with Kat, then pushed it out
of his head. Not exactly what Billy meant by visualizing.
Get in the now. Enjoy the moment. He'd get off, but it
would seem like just another workout.

SEVENTEEN

He was hungover at church. But the songs soothed him and the only time his head hurt was when he had to stand up. The guest preacher was a big young guy fresh out of seminary who took Ecclesiastes 3:1–8 as the basis for his sermon: "To every thing there is a season." When he started talking about the baseball season, Mike tuned in. When the preacher veered off, talking about making a brand-new ball game of your life with Jesus as coach, Mike tuned out. Same old.

He had liked going to church when the five of them went together, before Tiffany started spinning out of control and Scotty left for college. They had felt like a family then. That was a long time ago. He was just starting out in Little League, so he would have been eight years old. Tiffany would have been thirteen, not yet sneaking off to get piercings, and Scotty fifteen, spending most of his life wrapped around his cello. The three of them weren't that close; Scotty was too busy with his chamber music group to be a big brother and Tiffany was already on her own planet, but they got along well enough and never ratted each other out.

The first store had just opened then. Lots of new houses needed floors. Dad thought that going to church was a way to meet potential customers and get to know other merchants and politicians in the area. He was right. There would be a social hour after the service, and then the five of them would usually go to lunch at the fancy restaurant at the Ridgedale Inn or the big Greek diner on Route 17. In both places Dad would walk around, shaking hands and slapping backs. Mike could order whatever he wanted. Almost always hamburger and fries. Mom and Scotty were adventurous, fish dishes, pasta. Tiffany might pick at a vegetarian plate. It was fun.

He thought they might actually eat out to celebrate the first time in a long while they had been to church, but Dad pulled in at a deli in the mall and bought sandwiches to take to the new store.

In a couple of weeks it would be ready to open. A tiled walkway led under the arched SEMAK'S FABULOUS FLOORS sign into a huge, two-story building filled with areas for wall-to-wall carpeting, expensive throw rugs, and different kinds of tiles. Flat-screen TVs on the wall were running infomercials for different floor covering brands. Pretty fancy.

The store still smelled of paint and paste. Upstairs, men were spackling and hammering. In one corner, three dark-skinned men were sanding and staining wood flooring. One of them, tall, lanky, with a wispy mustache and goatee, jumped up to shake Dad's hand and thank him in broken English.

He and Dad talked in halting bursts of English and Spanish, and shook hands again. The man looked happy.

Walking back downstairs, Dad said, "This is what you got to deal with to get help. Ferdy lives in Orange County in New York, no car, and depends on his cousin to drop him off here. He can be here by eight A.M. but he needs to leave by six sharp for a second job in the city cleaning offices."

"Illegal?" Why did I say that, Mike thought.

Dad looked at him as if he were also wondering. "Illegal's a crummy word. These guys are willing to work hard, show up on time, clean, sober, cheerful. Grateful. What's so illegal about that?" Dad was almost shouting. "They're trying to survive."

"I got it." Mike raised his hands.

"He's here with his son, who goes to your high school, sending money back to the family in the Dominican Republic, trying to get them all together. . . ." He stopped.

"Sorry, Mike. Didn't mean to unload on you." He reached across Mike's shoulders and hugged him. "Really glad we can spend a little time together. It's all going to be yours someday. If we can hold on to it."

Mom approached with a spreadsheet and a frown. She and Dad disappeared into the back office. Be yours someday. He remembered driving Scotty to the airport after Christmas, the last time he had seen him. Scotty was happy to be going back to school. They talked about the new store and Scotty told him not to get trapped if he didn't want to spend the rest of his life looking down at the floor instead of up at the sky. It was very poetic and Mike knew Scotty wasn't thinking about the sky over center field.

EIGHTEEN

Coach Cody yanked Mike off the cafeteria line and steered him down the hall and into an empty classroom. "Talk to me. Saturday."

It took him a moment to dial into what Coach wanted. In his mind Saturday was Kat at the twins' party. "Same as last time. The senior center in Bergen Falls. Helping them get online."

"You got to do better than that."

"Coach, if I knew what you were looking for . . ."

"If I knew I'd know, right?" Coach's face was so close Mike could see the outlines of his contact lenses. Why does that surprise me? Everybody wears contacts, why not Coach? Somehow he thought Coach wouldn't need anything corrected. "I need to know what's going on in that club."

"You think something's going on?"

It sounded dumb but Coach nodded seriously, as if it had

been a smart question. "I want to pinch it off before Zack hurts himself and other people. I hate to see a fine athlete like Katherine Herold involved. Can I count on you?"

"You want me to spy on them?"

But Coach kept nodding seriously. "I tend to think of it as long-range Ranger recon, behind the lines." He turned to check the door. "Between us, Mike, I think they're hacking into school files, maybe even changing grades and evaluations. I could bring in the FBI, but then I would be exposing a lot of innocent people to privacy invasion. Are you tracking me?"

Mike wasn't sure he was, but he nodded, stalling for time. Coach wants to protect Kat. So do I. Why do I need to protect Tigerbitch? She can take care of herself. This FBI stuff sounds like he's trying to scare people. What TV show are we on? I'll just tell him a little. You only know a little, Mak. "They're going to a conference in the city on Saturday."

"Be there."

"What about the hitting clinic?"

"This is more important."

Not to me, Mike thought.

Coach put a hand on his shoulder. "I'm not going to forget what you're doing for me, for the team, the school. Better get some lunch."

Mike went back to the cafeteria, confused. He needed to

work on his batting mechanics. Look at his average. Maybe Coach didn't care about him. Team has another center fielder. Mike was expendable. Spies die. Don't get paranoid.

"What'd he want?" asked Andy.

"He wants me to nark on the Cyber Club. He says they're hacking into school files."

"Maybe hacking into his files," said Andy. "He's afraid they'll find out Oscar is twenty-five years old, lives in the Bronx, and took money from a Yankee scout."

"Does insanity run in your family?" said Mike.

"Nah, they're old-fashioned, middle-of-the-roaders like you."

Mike was happy to get lost in Dr. Ching's new problem. When two bulldozers that start from opposite sides of a field and are moving at different speeds pass each other, they are five hundred yards from one side of the field. When they reach the opposite sides of the field, they turn around and head back. The second time they pass each other they are two hundred yards from the other side. How wide is the field?

One of the brainiacs asked if they should assume the bulldozers were traveling at a constant speed, and should they disregard turnaround time. Dr. Ching said, Yes, yes, and also ignore the drivers pausing to text message and shuffle their iPods. Dr. Ching was the *NCIS* of math teachers.

* * *

He ditched last period study hall for jocks and went to the basement. It took him a while to find the Cyber Club in the back of the building. Zack and Kat weren't there, but half a dozen kids he recognized from the last two Saturdays were hanging and tapping away. It looked like the varsity lounge without Exercycles or video games. Or muscles. An Asian girl waved at him. Nick Brodsky, the Goth kid, sauntered over in his super-cool rolling walk.

"Hey."

"What's happening?" said Mike.

"Not much," said Nick. "Trying to decide if we hack into the school or the Pentagon today."

Mike thought, Is this guy onto me and mocking me? He said, "School. There's a B in English I'd like changed to an A."

Nick laughed. "Get in line. How much longer you got to help out here?"

Mike shrugged. "Coach keeps extending my sentence."

"That's Cody. Likes to mess with people's heads, keep them off balance." He lowered his voice. "That's why he sent you here to spy on us."

His mouth was dry. Was Nick playing with him or was he suspicious? "That's what you guys think?" He wondered if Kat thought that.

"Sure. If he didn't hate Zack so much he would have buried you. Zero tolerance, remember?"

"Why does he hate him?" He noticed that the web tattooed on Nick's neck wove around one ear.

"He hates anything that challenges his control of the school."

"You sound like Andy."

"At least they agree on something. But Andy only talks the talk. Zack walks the walk."

"How?"

Nick grinned. Mike could see the stud in his tongue. "You interrogating me for Cody?" He shifted his shoulders the way he did just before he bumped the defensive back and ran around him.

Stay cool. "You got it. Next comes torture. Waterboarding."

"You think that's funny?" Nick took a step closer.

Does he want me to hit him? Mike swallowed the anger bubbling up. *BillyBuddBillyBuddBillyBudd*. "I do."

"Me, too." Nick laughed. "Just busting your chops. Zack has some great ideas."

"Kat seems to think so." He thought it was cool the way he got her name in.

"She's drinking the Kool-Aid all right. Some piece of work, Tigerbitch, huh?" He locked eyes. What's Nick fishing for, Mike wondered.

"Helluva miler," said Mike. "I was surprised to see her here."

"I'm here, you're here," said Nick. "Jock heaven."

He's not going to tell me anything, Mike thought. His cell beeped. Text from Lori. ?RU. He'd forgotten he promised to meet her before practice. She just wasn't on his radar. "Gotta jump. Where is Zack?"

"He had a student government meeting."

"Could you tell them I'll be coming on Saturday?"

"Cool."

NINETEEN

Tuesday's game against Glen Hills was a laugher. Everybody hit. Oscar drove in five runs with a triple and two singles. Ryan unloaded a monster three-run homer over the center-field fence into the Glen Mall. Swinging late, Mike managed to slap a single into right field and then get thrown out trying to stretch it into a double. He felt stupid but no one seemed to notice as Ridgedale piled up runs. He had two easy chances in center. He felt unsure about them both until he squeezed the ball. He realized he wasn't silently daring batters to hit to him. He wasn't playing as shallow as usual. He didn't want the ball. The one shot deep to left center that might have given him trouble, Oscar took on a dead run.

Craig had a one-hit shutout going into the bottom of the ninth. His pitch count was high and his fastball seemed to be losing steam, but he told Coach he had to finish.

He wanted that shutout. Be the second one in a row, his eighth as a varsity starter. He was going for the Ridgedale career shutout record. Coach nodded. He liked that kind of fire.

Craig walked the first batter and hit the second. Two on, nobody out.

Mike waved Ryan and Oscar farther out. Catch the long flies, go for the big outs, even if a run scores. Craig shook his head and waved them in. Go for the play at the plate. He wanted that shutout. Then he walked the third batter to load the bases.

Two relief pitchers warmed up behind the fence as Coach Cody and the catcher, Jimmy Russo, walked out to the mound. Coach took the ball from Craig and signaled Todd and Mike to join them. He was the only coach in the conference who brought the center fielder in for conferences at the mound. The spine of the team.

By the time Mike reached the mound, Craig was red-faced, kicking at the dirt with his heel. "I can get out of this," he said.

Coach nodded at Jimmy, Todd, and Mike. "Deal or no deal?" He was also the only coach who listened to what players said. But he still made the final decisions.

Jimmy didn't look at Craig. "He's getting tired."

"He's got eleven runs," said Todd. "Give him a chance."

Coach rubbed the ball. He said, "We need a tiebreaker. Mike?"

Mike felt Craig's eyes boring into him. "You said this is about finding out what's inside us, Coach, what we're capable of."

"Well said." Coach flipped the ball back to Craig. "You've got a good defense behind you, let them work." He turned and headed back to the dugout. Todd and Mike patted Craig and jogged back to their positions.

The fourth batter blooped a hanging curve over DeVon's head into short left. Oscar came racing in. He looked like he was going to catch it. The runners ran back to their bases. Mike, backing up Oscar, was close enough to see how he quickly checked the runners, pretended to catch the ball close to the ground, then let it drop in front of his glove.

Oscar scooped up the ball and fired it to DeVon, who stepped on third for the force-out and threw to Hector at second for the second out. Hector threw to first. They almost had a triple play.

Mike caught his breath. I could never have pulled that off. If Oscar isn't a pro he should be. What a play.

"Way to go, Oscar," bellowed Coach, clapping. The Ridgedale players were cheering.

Oscar grinned and shrugged. Playing humble, thought

Mike. C'mon, man, give him a break. Maybe he is humble. Helluva play.

Craig was the only one who wasn't cheering. He stood silently, glaring at Oscar, his shutout ruined. But he had two outs now, only a runner on first, and an 11–1 game. Wasn't winning more important than individual stats?

Craig lost it then, a wild pitch that sent the runner to second and another walk. He didn't wait for the relief pitcher, just dropped the ball and stomped off the field. Kevin Park, the closer, got the final out, an unassisted groundout to Mark Rapp at first.

Craig was sullen on the bus back to Ridgedale. He sat in the rear with Eric Nola and stared out the window. He refused to talk to Jimmy Russo, shaking off the chunky catcher as if he were refusing a signal.

Up front, Coach was talking to Oscar, who grinned and nodded. Mike, trying not to stare, had a sinking feeling about what they were talking about.

Andy said, "That was some play. I didn't know it was legal to purposely let the ball drop like that."

"You can't do it in the infield with bases loaded and no outs," said Ryan. "No rule about the outfield, though. Cool trick."

"Should have saved it for the play-offs," said Mike. "Word gets around." Why do I have to put Oscar down?

"This is better," said Ryan. "They'll never know what he'll do. Keep 'em off balance."

"Off balance," said Andy. "Welcome to Ridgedale High."

Todd started singing the Ridgedale school song and as the guys picked it up, the sound ricocheted around the bus. Ryan bellowed the words off-key. Andy leaned over the back of Mike's bus seat and whispered in his ear, "How many high school kids can pull off a play like that? Get your geek peeps to check those files."

He wasn't surprised when Oscar started Thursday's game in center field, but he still felt a little stab of pain when Coach read the lineup. Mike was in left field. He'd been dropped to seventh place in the batting order.

"Lineups are not written in stone," said Coach, standing in the middle of the locker room. His gaze seemed to linger on Mike. "Every job is open for competition."

The twins cheered as Mike and Ryan ran out on the field, side by side as usual, then fell silent as they separated, Mike to left, Ryan to right. Mike didn't look at Lori. He didn't want to see the sympathy on her face that he knew would be there. She was sensitive, she would feel for him. Even though he could tell that she was beginning to sense he was just going through the motions with her.

He felt wrong, out of place, in left field. He remembered

waking up in a motel bedroom on a family trip once with the panicky feeling, Where am I? He should be in the middle of the field, teammates on either side, the game directly in front of him. There was nobody on his right and the game was slanted off to his left. It looked different. He couldn't see the pitches clearly.

Suck it up, he thought, you're making too big a deal of this. It's not so hard, it's not like shifting to left field in some big league ballpark with strange angles and shadows and grandstands looming over you. Most of the ballparks in the conference have standard high school outfields. This isn't like shifting to the infield, not even as radical as moving from linebacker to safety like you did last season.

But I'm a center fielder.

You're a baseball player.

He looked over at Oscar, relaxed and loose, playing shallow, even shallower than Mike did. Maybe he's just better, he thought. He pushed that thought way. I just need to step up. Show Coach what I'm capable of.

Willie Lockett, the number-two pitcher, struggled for the first five innings but managed to give up only two runs. In the bottom of the fifth, Oscar led off with a double, stole third, and scored on Ryan's sacrifice fly. Mark Rapp singled.

At bat, Mike visualized the homer that would put them

ahead, win the game. He relaxed his body the way Billy did, waggled his bat to drain the tension, then froze. He let the first pitch go by, a fastball the ump called a strike, and swung too eagerly at a slider, punching it foul. He took a ball, then watched a changeup curve outside. The ump called it strike three. He was on deck two innings later, the score still 2–1, two on and two out, when Mark flied out to end the game.

He felt numb as he walked to the grandstand to wish Lori good luck. The twins were going to Boston for a week-end twirling competition. Nearby, Oscar was talking to two dark-skinned men in work clothes. One of them looked like the new installer in the second store, the one so grateful to Dad for the job. Ferdy. The one who's got a kid going to my high school.

That's Oscar's father, Mike realized. When he walked the twins to their car, he saw Oscar getting into an old white van with New York plates. They lived out of the state, out of the school district. Oscar shouldn't be in Ridgedale High, certainly not eligible to play sports, nowhere near center field.

TWENTY

Coach Cody beckoned him out of jock study hall on Friday and silently steered him toward the school psychologist's office. He'd forgotten he was supposed to see the shrink. He was surprised when Coach Cody unlocked the door and followed him inside. He locked the door behind them. Mike had never been in this office before. It was just big enough for a swivel chair, a desk, and a shabby old two-seat couch. No windows.

Coach pointed Mike to the couch, then dropped into the swivel chair. It squeaked.

Coach looked at him for a long time. Mike started to feel uncomfortable. He wanted to shift his position on the couch, sit up higher, but he felt the weight of Coach's stare pressing him down.

Finally Coach nodded and said, "I'm a certified guid-ance counselor, you know that?" When Mike shook his head, Coach Cody smiled and said, "There are lots of things people don't know about me. Don't need to know. I've seen things I hope you never see. I don't expect you to under-stand why I do some of the things I do in this school, but you better believe it's all about making sure you never have to go through what I went through."

He leaned back in the chair. It squeaked louder. He closed his eyes and sighed. His shaven bowling ball head seemed to sink into his shoulders.

"I'm waiving your session with the school psycholo-gist for now because I don't want you to have anything on your record that could damage your shot at a college scholarship."

He let that sink in. Mike remembered that Dad had said the visit with the shrink wouldn't go on his record if noth-ing else happened. Dad would have made sure of something like that. Was Coach playing him?

"You've got good grades. You're a good kid. But . . ." His eyes snapped open ". . . unless I'm convinced you've worked through this issue to my satisfaction, you will have to see the shrink."

"How do I work through this issue?" What issue? he thought. My slump?

"Show me you understand why Zack Berger and the Cyber Club are a clear and present danger to the well-being of Ridgedale High School."

He almost expected Coach to break out in a big grin. It was a joke, right? An Andy Baughman riff. Clear and present danger. Andy had brought over a DVD of that movie. Harrison Ford was the CIA agent hero. They'd watched it on the eighty-four-inch pull-down screen.

"How many fights you been in at Ridgedale?" said Coach.

"None."

"Right," said Cody. "But this little smart-ass punk pushes your button. Gets you to hit him, make himself a martyr, draw attention to his cause. Classic." Cody's lips peeled back from his big white teeth. Mike could see where his gums were receding. "Meanwhile, your game goes into the tank. You lose focus because you're thinking about all this extraneous stuff. Your concentration's gone. Zack Berger's the reason you're in left field."

"What about Oscar?"

"He can play, no doubt," said Coach. "Might even have pro potential. But he's not a team leader. You're a team leader. You belong in center field, in the spine. And I want you back there."

Mike felt dizzy. He hadn't slept well, thinking about the third strike he took yesterday. He imagined himself in the middle of a math problem, only there was no answer. No clear and present answer. What is coach driving at?

"Semak? You still with me?"

"Yes, sir. I guess I just don't get it about Zack."

"Good guys always have a problem understanding just how insidious the bad guys are," said Coach. He swiveled and squeaked. "Zack's got an agenda. He hates authority, order, justice. You know, there are basically two kinds of guys in the world, jocks and pukes. We're jocks. We want to live by the rules, win fairly, work hard, and be rewarded for it. The pukes want to rebel and disrupt so they can slide through the chaos. Are you tracking me?"

Mike nodded.

"There are also different kinds of jocks. Your pal Ryan, steady, dependable, not much fire. You'll never get much more than you see. He's afraid to open up, let loose, go for the gold. He deflects everything with humor. He'll never rise high."

Coach was smiling, but he seemed to be smiling to himself, Mike thought, enjoying the sound of his voice. "Craig, lots of heat, but inconsistent emotionally, not dependable. Sure he can be terrific, but he can also be a disaster.

"And you. People might think you're like Ryan, always on an even keel, in control. But I know there's a fire in your belly, Mike, you can explode when you need to. Do what needs to be done. I like that. But I want to be sure you're exploding for the right reasons. Still tracking?"

Mike nodded again, but he wasn't sure any of it made sense.

"I know that ankle hurts like hell. I saw how you sucked it up in football. That tells me a lot. You remind me of a kid I knew when I was a Little League coach in Colorado. I've never told this story in this school, but I know it will be meaningful to you. This kid was steady and cool on the outside, you'd think he was a blank. But inside, that boy burned to do well, to compete, to win. Like you. Kid's name was William Budzinksi. Wonder what ever happened to him."

Mike's breath caught. "You coached Billy Budd?"

"Coached against him. Walked him a lot, let me tell you. This was just before his dad changed the family name. I don't even know if he actually read the Melville book. Billy Budd dies at the end. But Dad must have figured Billy Budd would sell a lot more of those batting gloves and wristbands you wear than William Budzinski."

Coach leaned back, shook his head at the ceiling. "Some world. We were on the same field and now he's in Yankee Stadium, one of the biggest superstars in the game, and I'm here at—" He stopped himself and looked at his watch. "You better get to practice."

Oscar worked out at shortstop with Coach Sherman while the rest of the team ran wind sprints and took extra batting

practice to prepare for tomorrow's clinic. Mike found himself watching Oscar scooping up grounders. Billy Budd
worked out at shortstop during spring training. Good for
your footwork. A lot of similarities between shortstop and
center field. Mickey Mantle started out a shortstop.

After practice he went into the new weight room with
Ryan. They spotted each other. They'd been lifting together
since middle school, when Ryan's dad set up a bench and
barbells in his garage.

"I think Coach's playing with me," said Mike.

"I'm trying to get Ms. Marsot to play with me," said Ryan.
"You believe these mopes who rat out their teachers after
they have sex?"

"I'm serious. He wants me to spy on the Cyber Club to
get back to center field."

"Cruise with it. Tell him everything." Ryan settled
under the bar. "Just don't tell him about us on Brokeback
Mountain."

For an instant Mike wanted to let the bar drop on Ryan's
leering face. Can't you be serious for one second and listen
to me? But maybe he just couldn't. Afraid to open up, let
loose. Coach was right about Ryan. Wonder if he's right
about me and Billy.

There were voice and text messages from Lori. She was
in Boston and she was nervous. The twins were going to

do a fire stick routine they had never done in competition before. The other girls had awesome routines. Tori had a sinus infection that was throwing her off. Please call me.

He called. Need to talk to somebody. He got her voice mail. He wasn't sure if he was sorry or glad.

Not sure of much these days, are you?

He watched the Yankees game downstairs. The cat sat across the room and glared at him. He wouldn't have minded if she climbed into his lap. You really must be lonely, Mike.

Billy's timing seemed off, he was hitting on top of the ball, choppers instead of his usual line drives. But some of them were going through for base hits. Even when he's off, he's on. Mike heard the garage door opening. He didn't feel like talking to his parents. He got up. The cat swiped at his bare foot as he passed. Nicked him.

In his room, on the Buddsite, he read EmoBaller's theory that Billy was being distracted by that model. Catchergrrl reminded him how Billy had played out of his skull the week his grandma died, setting a record for postseason hits. As usual, EmoBaller agreed with her.

An alert popped up. The A Day With Billy contest closes Sunday, right after the doubleheader! Get those videos in! He wondered if Coach had really known Billy in Little League. Would Coach make up something like that to motivate me? To play better? To spy for him? Could be. But not a lot of people knew about that name change. Nothing about it on the Buddsite. Mike had read about it once, years ago in a baseball magazine, then it never came up again. He wondered what Coach had been about to say when he said, "and I'm here at . . ." Did he wish he were somewhere else?

Lori still wasn't answering her phone. For a moment he thought about calling Andy. Talk about Coach's jock-puke theory. What's that all about? But Andy would turn it into a lecture on politics. He realized he didn't really have anyone else to talk to. But what did he have to say?

The cat scratch on his foot stung. He thought of Tigerbitch. I'll see her tomorrow.

TWENTY-ONE

Kat drove the van toward the city, swiftly, confidently, one hand on the steering wheel, the other gesturing at Zack, who sat shotgun, tapping on his laptop. Mike couldn't hear most of what they were saying. It sounded more political than personal. He wondered if she was driving too fast as she gunned out of a toll booth. But she seemed in control, happy.

Mike was in the third row between two pukey-looking guys, one fat, one skinny, who were text messaging each other. How had he gotten between them? He had climbed into the van and suddenly they had appeared, one at each door, and sandwiched him. He didn't think they meant to do it, they just did it in that uncool dorky way. A jock might let a classroom door close on you, but never by accident. He thought he had seen these two around school, but it could have been two other kids who looked like them, wore lame band T-shirts, and walked on their heels. He never paid much attention to geeks and nerds. When jocks gave them a hard time, he walked away. He felt bad one time when some football players trash-canned a puke, stuffed him into one of the cafeteria garbage baskets. He thought that Billy would have stopped the bullying, but Mike didn't feel strong enough. Maybe didn't care enough. Coach was right. Pukes are different.

In the bench seat in front of them, a Chinese kid was sleeping against the window and Nick the Goth was leaning into a girl with a Mohawk and nose rings. She wasn't bad-looking. He hadn't talked to Nick this morning when they met at the van. Still trying to figure him out. Does he really think I'm a spy for Cody, or is he pulling my chain?

They crossed the bridge and Kat swung the van down an exit ramp into the city. The Hudson River sparkled on their right as tall apartment houses loomed on the left. The city always made him a little nervous. It seemed dangerous, mysterious. They had rarely traveled in as a family except for the occasional Yankee game or Broadway show. There were class trips to museums. There were kids who went to dance clubs in the city, a druggie crowd he avoided.

Tiffany had disappeared into the city for a couple of days

when she was fifteen. Mom and Dad freaked. When the police brought her back, she'd seemed different, spacey. Mike was too busy playing ball to pay much attention, but he remembered her fighting with Mom, screaming, doors slamming. Scotty had just left for college. Now he was in Indiana and she was a single mom living in the East Village with her little daughter. And I'm in left field. Remembering that made his stomach ache.

The pukes on each side of him started laughing through their noses at something they were messaging back and forth. Mike was getting more and more frustrated between them. He was too large for this group. If they were jocks he would have elbowed some more space for himself. If they were jocks the van would be noisy and friendly. Mike started digging into a pocket for his iPod, trying not to poke them.

He heard Nick say, "Ask him yourself. He's house-broken." When the girl murmured something, Nick turned around and said, "Syl wants to know why you're here."

Tell her I'm spying for Coach Cody. Mike put on a tough *Law & Order* voice. "Zack thought you needed security."

The fat kid snorted, thumbs flying, and a moment later the skinny kid laughed so hard Mike thought he was going to choke. Smart-ass pukes.

The Chinese kid turned around. He'd only been pretending to sleep. "You take steroids?"

"You take smart pills?" said Mike.

"You got any?" said Nick. He was laughing. "Smart pills are the only ones I never took."

"Figured," said Syl.

The Chinese kid turned to Nick. "You took steroids?"

Mike thought, I'm in a reality show. An alternate universe. These people are weird. They are definitely not housebroken.

"I took them one summer before football camp," said Nick. "It helped a little I think but you need to be a physical freak like Mike here for it to do any real good. And then you have to lift like crazy. I never cared that much."

"You were a football player?" The fat kid's fingers were frozen in midair.

"He was a good receiver," said Mike. "I couldn't keep up with him."

"Thanks." Nick looked pleased. "Maybe I should've worked harder. I couldn't deal with those fascist coaches."

"The suppression of any dissent," said Syl.

I'll channel Andy, thought Mike. "It's all about keeping us off balance and maintaining totalitarian control." He thought he had said it sarcastically, but the way Syl and the others nodded and seemed to look at him differently, he realized they thought he was serious.

Except maybe Nick. He had a smirk on his face. Either he wasn't totally buying or he was giving Mike a hard time. "So, comrade, how come you decked Zack?"

"He wouldn't get out of my way."

The Chinese kid said, "Why didn't they suspend you?"

"Rules are not for stars," said Nick. "If you're as good as Mike you do what you want."

They were driving past Chelsea Piers now. The varsity and JV had gone there for last year's hitting clinic with Dwayne Higgins, the Yankees' right fielder. There was a rumor Billy would show up to support his bud but he didn't. Higgins mostly talked about himself. The minor league coaches who came with Dwayne gave the high school players batting tips and actually worked on individual stances and swings. One of the coaches said Mike needed to get his hips open sooner. He had worked on that and it helped. He wondered what good advice he was missing today at the Meadowlands. Maybe some tip that could get him back into center field. But according to Coach, that's not what will get me back.

If I understood what Coach was talking about.

Mike followed Zack and the others into an old factory building near the river while Kat screeched off to park the van. A hundred kids, mostly high school guys, were packed into an auditorium. The kids seemed pretty psyched by what they were hearing, tech jargon Mike had trouble following. They recorded, videotaped, and made notes in their laptops as speakers up front droned on about something called On-High dot org that was going to revolutionize education in America by making high schools accountable to the students. That part Mike understood but not how they were going make it all happen with the help of backdoors and packets and sniffers and tunneling. Speakers made jokes about scooters and pinheads. Mike sat behind Fatty and Skinny, who laughed and elbowed each other continually. Mike got some of the *Matrix*, *Star Wars*, and *Battlestar Galactica* references, but that didn't help much since the speakers seemed to think that was all ancient culture anyway. He kept looking around for Kat but didn't see her.

He became alert when Zack got up to speak. The crowd seemed to know and respect him.

"High school is a prison and Ridgedale is maximum security," he said.

The crowd howled. Fatty and Skinny bumped foreheads. I'm in a nuthouse, Mike thought. Nick was whistling and cheering Zack on.

"We're running a two-pronged operation right now,

an outreach program to bring in marginalized users, older folks and disabled teenagers, that's being funded by the school board. That money's also helping expand our internal operation. We have a site called Ridgedale-Reform dot org making students aware of how we're being controlled by the system, where the money goes, and how educational decisions are made against our best interests."

Zack was getting excited now, talking faster. Mike could see the spittle forming in the corners of his mouth. He remembered their confrontation in the hallway.

"We've got chat rooms on Ridgedalesucks dot com that disseminates information on teachers and students, particularly certain government types and the jockocracy, how athletes run the school." Mike remembered Craig and Eric complaining in the locker room about something they'd read online about favoritism in grading for jocks. Mike had barely paid attention. Craig wanted to trash can the Cyber Club but Todd had talked him out of it.

"We're constructing a new site, Codywatch dot com. Cody is our vice principal."

"The head Cylon," yelled Fatty. Skinny looked like he was wetting his pants.

"Hack Cody," shouted Nick.

"That's the plan," said Zack. "We're going to expose him,

drill into his . . ." He stopped himself, as if he thought he might be going too far. He took a breath, went back to his deep, even voice. "I know a lot of other schools have similar programs and if we all link up with On-High dot org we will be invincible."

Nick leaped up and thrust a fist into the air. Other kids stood up and cheered. This was what Cody was talking about, the clear and present danger. Coach wasn't entirely paranoid. Am I supposed to tell him about this? What about Kat?

Mike stood up and scanned the room until he found her, crouching along a wall, shooting video of Zack. He watched her. She was graceful and quick. Like a cat, he thought. When she turned her head, her ponytail bobbed through the back of her baseball cap.

Watching her took his breath away, pushed out other thoughts.

The lead speakers took over then, quieted them down, and started talking about committees and networks. The meeting broke up. Zack and a dozen other kids stayed up front talking. Kat stood a few feet away, shooting them. Mike walked up to her casually. The way she looked over her shoulder and smiled, he had the sense she had been waiting for him.

* * *

"I'm walking over to the East Village," she said. She held up her camera. "I want to shoot some stuff." She was wound up, full of energy.

"I'm actually heading in that direction, too," he said. "My sister lives there." He didn't want her to think it was about her, even if she looked oddly excited.

TWENTY-TWO

They walked for a long time, through Tribeca and Chinatown and Little Italy, stopping for Kat to shoot, and then into a huge restaurant on Houston Street called Katz's.

"Best deli in the world," said Kat.

It was crowded, noisy, and dingy. He didn't feel so hungry anymore. There were fading signs on the wall. SEND A SALAMI TO YOUR BOY IN THE ARMY! Was that supposed to be a rhyme? And which war, he wondered. Sharp, spicy smells brought his appetite back.

Kat led him to a counter where grumpy men were slicing huge hunks of fatty meat. She said, "You have to try the pastrami and corned beef." She seemed so sure of herself. She ordered two sandwiches, extra pickles, cream soda. One of the men punched Kat's ticket.

They carried the food to a greasy table. "You see the movie *When Harry Met Sally?*"

He nodded. Tori and Lori loved it, made him and Ryan

watch it with them and then talk about whether men and women could be friends. Ryan had said it was impossible. Mike had no opinion. He hoped Kat wasn't going to ask him about that.

She pointed to a table where a couple were laughing. "In the movie, that's where Meg Ryan did her fake orgasm. Remember?"

He did. That scene had embarrassed him and Ryan. Lori and Tori thought it was hilarious and did their own imitations.

"You come here a lot?" As soon as he realized he had made a pun he felt heat rise in his neck.

She laughed loudly and slapped the table. He'd never seen her so up. "That's pretty good for"—she flashed the smile—"a dumb jock." She split the sandwiches. "I like them both so if you don't, we can switch back."

He didn't like either of them, thick, tangy meats that fell into his gut like lumps of fat. The cream soda tasted like dessert. He didn't like that either, but he smiled and nodded as if it were pizza and Dr Pepper. He watched her eat. She didn't nibble at her food like Lori, she really dug in. There was grease around her lips. He relaxed.

"And you were giving Andy a hard time for a cheese-burger."

"Nobody's perfect." She laughed and talked with her mouth full. "Besides, I hardly ever eat like this."

"What are you shooting?"

"It's a project for Social Issues." The sharp edges of her face seemed to soften. "I want to shoot a lot of faces, different generations, races, ethnic types, then match them up in a montage." The words spilled out rapidly, almost breathlessly. He was caught up in her high spirits. "I want to show how people are more similar than different."

"You believe that?"

"Don't you?"

"Never thought about it."

"Neither did I until I hurt my knee and had to stop running," she said. "I was really down. Everything was about track till then. You know, when you're running hard you're not looking around at the world. You're so focused in competition, you can avoid everything else."

"Tell me about it," he said.

"I started talking to Zack and reading websites he suggested, and I got out of myself. Saved my life." She said it matter-of-factly.

He wanted more. "Saved your life?"

"Literally. I was . . ." She stopped. "Some other time." She jammed the sandwich into her mouth. With her mouth full, she said, "You close to your sister?"

"My sister?" It took him a moment to remember he had mentioned his sister back in the auditorium. "Not really.

She left home when I was about eleven."

"She a lot older than you?" Kat looked interested. Or maybe she was just changing the subject.

"She's twenty-two. When she was around sixteen she kind of went crazy, had like a breakdown. Drugs and stuff." He talked fast. He had never told anyone this much about Tiffany before. Or about anything this personal, really. He wondered why he was now. "They needed to kidnap her out of the house and take her to a camp in Utah to straighten out."

Kat winced. "How long was she there?"

"Almost three years. There and another place."

Kat looked as if she were in pain. "It all worked out?"

"I guess so. She's got a job, her own apartment, a daughter."

"She's married?"

"No."

"You and your parents see her?"

"Yeah, we come in, she comes out to the house with the kid for holidays, but everybody's pretty busy these days."

She looked serious. "Just don't lose that relationship."

He wondered why this all seemed so important to her. What did it have to do with her? He kept pushing the sandwich into his mouth. He didn't want her to think he didn't like it.

After a while, to get the conversation started again, he

said, "You running this season?"

It took her a moment, as if his question had come over a satellite phone from a different continent, like in live TV news. But when her head came up, she seemed happy to answer. "I don't know. I'm pretty far behind in my training. And I've been thinking a lot about why I started to run in the first place."

"Why did you?"

She looked at him as if the answer were obvious. "So I could blot everything out. When I run hard, I don't think of anything else, don't feel anything except the pain in my body."

He thought of the Ranger Runs. *Was that why I liked them so much?*

When they finished, Kat turned in their tickets and paid. Mike tried to give her money, but she brushed it aside. "Yours next time."

He liked that. Next time.

They walked to a park along the East River. Latino families were barbecuing and playing ball. She moved among them, asking for permission to shoot them. She was friendly but bold. They smiled at her. *No problemo.*

While she shot, Mike sat on a bench, watching her and the games. A lot of talented ballplayers. Some of them looked like Oscar. After a while she joined him on a bench.

"Andy said you were pissed because that new Dominican kid took over center field."

"Andy talks a lot."

"Is it true?"

He felt defensive. "I wasn't pissed because he was Dominican."

"I didn't mean that," she said quickly, putting a long, slim hand on his arm. He was sorry when she took it away. "I remembered what you said about center field at the senior center. It was so poetic."

"Just babbling. I felt stupid."

"It was great." She gave him a funny little smile. "I should send it to Billy Budd. He'd love it. Even Zack was blown away."

"Right."

"You know, Zack was embarrassed by what happened between you two. He's not like that. He gets intense, but he's not a total jerk. He just doesn't have social skills. He really cares about what he's doing."

He blurted, "You two, um, like going together?"

She shook her head. "I'm not into that these days."

They wandered the East Village. Mike enjoyed just being with her, watching her quick, smooth movements as she spun in and out of crowds to shoot. He imagined the body under the warm-up suit. She shot an Indian family and black basketball players. A junkie started hassling her, backed off when Mike stepped between them. She looked grateful. Dumb jock bodyguard, he thought. Everybody needs one.

They stopped at an outdoor café for coffee and cake. There were other couples. He felt like they were one.

"How's your ankle?"

It took him a moment to remember his sore ankle. "It's been okay. Your knee?"

"I'm starting to put some weight on it. We should run."

"If I can keep up."

She wrote something on a piece of napkin and gave it to him. "Call me when you feel like running. Really just jogging for now."

She looked at her watch. "I better call Zack. We're supposed to meet up about now, to go home. It's his van, but he hates to drive in the city."

He nodded. He wasn't ready for the day to end.

"You said you're meeting your sister, right?"

He felt caught in the lie. "Right." He paid the check. He hoped it wasn't the only next time.

"That was fun," she said. She kissed him on the cheek before she jogged away. He couldn't move until she was out of sight. He was confused. Is she coming on to me?

* * *

He thought about calling Tiffany. Or just ringing her door-
bell. She lived in a walk-up apartment with her daughter,
Sophia, who was almost four. Mom had seen them a couple
of weeks ago. She called the apartment a dump. But she
had to admit that Tiffany, for once, seemed happy. She had
a waitress job nearby and a friend who babysat. He liked
Tiffany and Sophia, but he didn't have much to say to
them.

He circled Tiffany's block twice, trying to walk off the
chunks of fat hardening in his stomach and decide whether
or not to ring her bell. He knew she would be glad to see
him, but then what? Be embarrassing. Somehow he knew
Kat would ask him about his sister when he saw her again
and he didn't want to lie.

The downstairs buzzer had an OUT OF ORDER sign and
while he stared at the T. Semak label with its smiley face,
a guy unlocked the lobby door and let him in. He walked
up three flights of shabby stairs. Food and pot smells roiled
his stomach, disturbing the fat chunks. He knocked on
Tiffany's door. He could hear the TV inside. Sounded like
a kid's cartoon.

"Yeah? Who?" It didn't sound like her. The peephole
clicked open.

"It's Mike. I was just in the neighborhood. . . ."

"I recognize you." The door opened and a squat person in a sweatshirt and jeans was grinning at him. Buzz-cut blond hair. He couldn't tell if it was male or female. "The baseball brother, right? Your picture's on her screensaver. I'm her friend, Arlene." She grabbed his hand and pumped. Strong grip. "She's working. Wanna come in?"

"No, thanks, I gotta go. Just tell her I stopped by."

"Say hello to Sophia?"

"Next time, I'll come back." He sidestepped down the hall, waving at Arlene until he got to the stairs, turned and hurried down. What's wrong with you? You could've said hello to the kid. Then what? You afraid of Arlene? Probably wanted to talk ball. Bet she's a Yankee fan, too.

I just didn't want to get out of the mood, he thought. I got Kat on my mind. That's enough right now.

He walked all the way to Times Square and took a bus home. He turned on his cell. There were texts from Lori. He felt as though he had been cheating on her. She'd want to know about today. Not going to tell her about Katz's for sure. His mind felt jumbled. What was he going to tell Cody? He didn't care about the pukes, but he didn't want Kat to get involved.

TWENTY-THREE

Mom and Dad had come home late from the new store on Saturday night and went back early Sunday morning, leaving him notes and food he couldn't eat. He woke Sunday to his stomach churning. Was it still the strange meats at Katz's or everything else? Kat. Center field. What was he going to tell Coach on Monday? It wasn't just about ratting out Zack and the Cyber Club, it would be ratting out Kat.

He wished he understood her. He needed to talk to her. Carefully, he opened the napkin she had written on. He had two false starts before he took a deep breath and punched her numbers.

"Huh?" She sounded like she had been asleep.

"I wake you?"

She hung up.

He called back.

"Wha?" Asleep or drugged, he thought.

"It's Mike."

"Mike."

"I thought you might like to run. Take a break, clear your head."

There was a pause. "I was up all night. Editing. On deadline."

"The Social Issues Project?"

"I'll tell you sometime." She sounded cold, far away. She hung up.

Probably something for Zack. Something they didn't trust him with knowing. He felt rejected. She didn't sound at all like the girl he had been with yesterday. Had she changed her mind about a next time or had that kiss been a goodbye not a come-on? Hey, Mak, it's not always about you. He remembered what Tori had said about mood swings. But maybe it was his call that had swung her mood into the toilet.

He took a long bike ride to the community college track, the best in the county, and tested the ankle at different speeds. He ran backward and sideways. It seemed okay.

On the way back he stopped at Andy's house. As usual, Andy's parents were glad to see him. They thought he was a good influence. They insisted he stay for dinner. He lied and said his parents were expecting him. Andy was in his room with the door locked. He opened it a crack when Mike pounded, then let him in quickly. He was watching a debate on C-Span.

"I need to talk to you," said Mike.

"What about?" Andy switched to alert mode. He loved new information.

"Coach is on my back. To spy on the Cyber Club. He wants evidence that they're hacking into school files, that they're doing stuff to undermine the administration."

"Are they?"

"Sounds like it."

"Best thing I ever heard about them."

"I don't know what to do." As soon as he said it, he felt better. The churning slowed. Billy said that sometimes you need a friend to share your problems. It's okay to ask for help.

"You don't owe those lefties anything."

"I'm not a snitch," said Mike.

"It's not snitching, it's counterterrorism. Jack Bauer in 24, best show on the tube."

"C'mon. You're the guy calls Coach some kind of dictator."

"Sometimes you need one. You think Oscar's the only illegal in school?"

"Coach brought him in." His stomach started churning again.

"There you go," said Andy. "Need I say more?"

"You're not making any sense. Whose side are you on?"

"You got to play all sides. You think Oscar just kind of wandered into Ridgedale, 'Hola, amigos, you got a béisbol team?'" Andy laughed to himself. "Cody recruited him. Found him somewhere, got him set up. Maybe a job for a member of his family."

Mike thought of Ferdy. Had Coach talked to Dad about hiring him? Part of the deal they cut after he pushed Zack?

Andy said, "So what was it the geeks were talking about?"

"Something called On-High dot org. Kids from different schools sharing information."

"That would scare old Cody. And a lot of other people. Especially once the kids put up stuff they've hacked. The next terrorist attack is going to come from cyberspace."

"You heard of Ridgedalesucks dot com?"

"Sure." Andy flopped down at his desk and tapped on his laptop. Mike watched over his shoulder as Ridgedalesucks .com came up. It was a flashy website, but most of the columns and posts were attacks on individual teachers for being boring, giving low grades, or smelling bad. There were whiny complaints about fungi in the basement, rat feces in the cafeteria, and dangerous conditions in the chem lab. The sports column was mostly rants about jocks getting grades they didn't deserve and acting like assholes in the hallway. There was an item about a star pitcher who might be taking steroids when he wasn't busy getting drunk at his parties.

"That's Craig," said Andy. "Probably true."

"Try Codywatch."

Coach in his camo filled the screen. It looked like a cell phone picture of the photo in his office. Up close, the hard, tough grin was intimidating. Underneath it read: "Who is this man?" There wasn't much on the site yet, except Cody's résumé on file with the school board and a call for information and opinions.

"This is pretty pathetic for an underground site," said Andy.

"They're just getting started," said Mike.

"You get to hang out with Tigerbitch?"

Mike shook his head no. He wanted to talk about her, but not right now with Andy.

On Monday he felt numb and nervous waiting for Cody to summon him out of class and grill him about Saturday. He still didn't know what he was going to say. At lunch Lori barely talked to him. She pretended she couldn't tear loose from her latest vampire novel. She's rejecting me, too, he thought, but I don't care. Tori and their mom had gone into the city to see a specialist about Tori's sinus infection.

It had made her too shaky to do their fire dance routine with its flaming sticks over the weekend. Their devil stick routine, which wasn't as spectacular or dangerous, got them second place to a couple of girls they thought they should have beaten. Mike had the feeling that Lori was pissed at him for not answering her calls.

Dr. Ching's class worked through the equations to solve the bulldozer problem. The first one was the width of the field equals the time until the bulldozers first passed convoluted with the sum of the two bulldozers' speed. It wasn't that hard but Mike couldn't focus. He watched the door for Cody. He thought, There is no one I can talk to.

At practice the coaches reviewed the hitting clinic. It had been a good one. Mike felt left behind. Coach Cody never even looked at him. He spent most of the time working with Oscar on his follow-through. One of the pro coaches had brought it up at the clinic.

After practice Mike lifted for an hour to drain off the energy buzzing in his body. By the time he rode out of the varsity lot, rain clouds had gathered, darkening the early evening.

He was on a quiet side street with no sidewalks, riding close to tall bushes hiding the houses on the other side, when he sensed a car slowly coming up behind him. He held the bike steady to let it pass.

He heard an angry curse and turned in time to see spiky black hair and a tattooed neck through the passenger window of a white van. The door opened and became a metal wall that slammed him off his bike. The van sped away.

TWENTY-FOUR

He scrambled up yelling, looking for a rock to throw. The van careened around a corner. By the time he untangled the bike from the bushes alongside the road and took off after the van, it was out of sight.

Deep breaths. A dozen *BillyBudds*. He shivered all the way home. He'd fallen off his bike before, even been run off the road a couple of times. But this was different. This was personal.

It had looked like Nick in the Cyber Express. Zack's van. Why?

And who was driving?

His mind felt like a car engine being braked and accelerated at the same time, snarling, whirring, going nowhere.

He didn't know if he was glad or sorry no one was home. He didn't want anyone to see he was still trembling, but he wanted someone to talk to.

He fed the cat and changed her water for something normal to do. His right shoulder felt sore when he stretched his arm.

What's wrong with you, Mike? You've taken hard hits before. You've had your bell rung in football.

That was different, he thought. That was a game.

His hands stung from scrapes. He went into the bathroom to check his face, which was beginning to sting, too. A few long scratches on his right cheek. Good thing he'd been wearing his helmet.

He nuked the dinner Mom had left and took it upstairs.

Think this through.

It had looked like the Cyber Express, looked like Nick. But it happened too fast to be sure of anything. Eyewitness accounts were often faulty on the crime shows. Where's the evidence? And what was the motive? The sharp-faced, sexy cops and assistant DAs who looked like Kat always asked those questions.

Kat. Would she know who was in the van? What was the big secret project she couldn't talk about yesterday?

He sent her a text. Wassup?

His cell beeped almost immediately. It was Lori. She wanted him to call right away.

It was a long, boring, one-sided conversation. Her words were slurred. She'd taken a pill to calm herself down. She was sorry she'd been so cranky at lunch, but she'd been bummed about Boston. Not being able to do the fire sticks routine had set back their schedule leading to the national championships. He knew she was as dedicated to twirling as he was to baseball, that she had always been willing to listen to him even though he never actually said that much. But he could barely concentrate. All he could think about was the white van. He felt sad that he didn't want to talk to her about it. He was grateful when she started to mumble, realized she was falling asleep, apologized, said she loved him, and hung up before he had to say anything to her.

He was calmer now. The shaking had stopped.

He had more than a dozen texts and voice mails. None were from Kat. There were three missed calls from a blocked number. Just before he shut off his cell, he answered the fourth call from a blocked number. He thought he could hear breathing on the other end, but after the third time he said, "Hello?" the phone went dead. He thought it sounded like Kat's breathing. That's nuts, he thought. When have you listened to her breathe? You just want it to be her.

Makes no sense. But it also makes no sense that Nick would door you.

Billy Budd looked down at him from the poster and said, *Get your mind into something else, young baller.* It was in his book. *Overanalysis can lead to paralysis.*

He found an old *Law & Order* he had only seen twice. His shoulder hurt and his ankle joined in. Excuse enough to take a Vic. He didn't pay attention to the show. He knew who the murderer was. He watched the way the detectives barked at suspects, so sure of themselves, and the way the female district attorney whipped her dark hair. He was drifting off to sleep when he heard his parents come home.

Usually, with a game that afternoon, he would have driven to school Tuesday morning. After a game, sweaty and beat, it was easier to jump in and take off than pedal home. But he didn't want to give Nick or whoever the satisfaction that he'd been scared off his bike. Don't mess with the Mak. What was he going to do when he caught up with the little bastard?

Something felt different in the halls. It took him two periods to realize it was the way the geeks and freaks were looking at him. Usually they turned their heads and gave jocks space. Today they were glaring and muttering. Somebody bumped him from behind on a stairway. When he got to his locker after the second period, he found a picture of a rat taped to the door.

Zack and the Chinese kid were absent from his history class. Kat wasn't in Social Issues. He looked for Nick. Nowhere. He had no idea what was going on until lunch.

Ryan said, "I got your back, man."

Lori sat down next to him. "I can't believe you let me go on and on last night, Mike." She squeezed his thigh under the table. "Thank you so much for being there for me."

"What's going on?"

Ryan said, "If you ever answered your cell or read your texts. . . ."

"Mr. Cody shut down the Cyber Club yesterday afternoon," said Tori. "Zack and everybody in the club are at the superintendent's office."

"Why?"

"Because somebody," said Andy, looking at Mike, "finally had the balls to stand up to those pukes."

TWENTY-FIVE

Before the game Coach Sherman said that Coach Cody was away on district business. Oscar was home with a sore hamstring. Mike Semak was starting in center field.

Mike felt as though he had just come back from the flu, finally clearheaded and pain free after days of misery, but still a little weaker than normal. Center field somehow seemed different, smaller, the grass scrubbier. He was trapped in a box. Had something changed?

He figured his first chance in the field would change it back, but it didn't. An easy fly to short center he hardly had to move to catch. He squeezed it hard, afraid it would pop out of his glove.

Over in left, Eric Nola shouted, "Way to go, Mak!" Nola was very happy to be back in the lineup. Mike looked over at Ryan, who threw him a fist. Mike thought, Did I look unsure of myself? Do they think I need encouragement to make a simple catch?

He didn't embarrass himself at bat, a walk and a single in four appearances, but he didn't distinguish himself either. It was a long, sloppy game. The sophomore first baseman who had replaced Andy hit a home run with two on, and Willie Lockett with Kevin Park in relief managed to keep Valley Hills from ever closing the gap.

In the locker room Craig swaggered over and threw an arm over Mike's shoulders. "Friday night barbie at my house after the game. Bring your twin." It was the first time he'd been invited to one of Craig's legendary parties.

Todd fist-bumped him. "You got my vote, Mike."

Andy caught up with him on his way out. "The Ridgedale idol. What's it feel like?"

"I didn't nark the Cyber Club."

"You are Jack Bauer," said Andy. "You should change your number to twenty-four."

Maybe you're Jack Bauer, thought Mike. I told you too much. Mike cursed and brushed past him.

Lori was waiting for him. The cheerleaders had just finished their practice. "We're going to Craig's," she said, almost jumping up and down. Tori was honking the car horn.

"How come everybody thinks they know my business?" His voice sounded whiny to him.

She just laughed at his scowl. "It's so funny, you never read your email, your webcam's never been activated, your cell is never on, no speed dial, you live back in the twentieth century, and you're the one to expose the Cyber Club." She went up on her toes to kiss him. "Call you later. Gotta go."

Dad's Lexus and an old white van were in the driveway. For a moment he thought it was the Cyber Express. Then he saw its New York license plates. Still, he was surprised to find Oscar and Ferdy at the kitchen table, drinking coffee with Mom and Dad.

Mom said, "Mike. I know you know Oscar, and this is his dad, Ferdy."

Ferdy stood up, wiped his hands on his jeans, and offered a hand to shake. It was hard and callused. Oscar looked up and nodded. He didn't look happy.

"How's your hamstring?" said Mike.

Oscar looked confused. "What?"

Dad cleared his throat. "As far as other people are concerned, Oscar and Ferdy will be, uh, staying with us for a while."

"How come?" said Mike.

Dad and Mom looked at each other. "Be closer to work and school," said Dad.

Ferdy looked at his watch and said something in Spanish.

Oscar stood up and said, "Later, man."

Mike watched them leave, Ferdy smiling, almost bowing his way out, Oscar swaggering off. He waited until he heard the van doors slam outside. "What the hell's going on?"

"Don't use that tone on me," snapped Dad.

"Easy, Scott."

"Yeah. Sorry." Dad looked sorry. "Trust me, this is more than you want to know." He looked at his watch, then at Mom. "We've got to get back. The accountant's coming over. Oh, one other thing." He pointed at a small blue duffel bag on the floor near the kitchen table. The name tag dangling from its handle said O. Ramirez. "Would you throw that in Scotty's room."

"Why?"

"Please," said Dad over his shoulder on his way out.

Mom pressed a twenty-dollar bill into his hand. "I'll explain everything later. It'll be fine. Don't worry about it. Get some pizza." She kissed him and followed Dad out. He watched her go out. Not like her at all. She thought he ate too much pizza. What the hell's going on?

He called Lori. She squealed. "I can't believe you called."

"The cat dialed for me," he said.

"I believe that. So now you have to tell me the whole story."

"I feel like I'm the only one who doesn't know it. What's going on?"

"Tori heard that Mr. Cody changed the locks on the Cyber Club's room, and he's got, like, the FBI searching through their hard drives."

"Why?"

"Oh, Mikey." She wailed. "Don't do this! They could torture me. I wouldn't tell anyone anything you told me."

"I didn't turn them in. I never gave Coach any incriminating information about the Cyber Club."

"Okay." She sounded disappointed. "Tori heard Mr. Cody boast to somebody that he had the Cyber Club right where he wanted them and we figured . . ."

"It wasn't me." He thought about Cody and Oscar both missing practice and then the Ramirezes showing up at his house. "Tori hear anything about Oscar Ramirez?"

"The district office was checking his address to see if he was eligible to attend Ridgedale. I think somebody complained."

"That wasn't me either."

"Nobody would blame you, you should be playing center field. . . ."

Another call was coming in. Somehow he knew it was Kat. "I got to go now, talk to you later." He clicked Lori off in mid sentence.

Before Kat had a chance to speak, he said, "Why'd you make those calls and hang up?"

"I wanted to know you weren't hurt." Her voice sounded tentative, almost afraid.

"How'd you know about the van?" He dreaded the answer.

"Nick told me." She clicked off.

TWENTY-SIX

It was almost midnight when he heard the Lexus roll into the driveway. The garage door hummed up, hummed down. Car doors opened, closed. His parents clattered through the garage into the kitchen. The refrigerator clicked open. Dad was having a beer. The laptop on the kitchen counter told Mom she had mail. He went downstairs.

"You're still up," said Mom. "Would you like something?"

"Some answers. What's going on?" She looked tired. He felt guilty sounding like the cops on *CSI*.

"You deserve answers," said Dad smoothly. "Tomorrow, when . . ."

"Tonight." It came out more harshly than he had intended.

Dad's head jerked up. Mom looked down at her laptop and said, "It's been a very long day and night and we . . ."

"Long for me, too. Everybody thinks I ratted out the Cyber Club."

Dad and Mom looked at each other. He said, "Did you?"

"How can you ask me that?" Mike was shouting.

"This isn't like you, Mike," said Mom soothingly, like she was calming an angry dog.

BillyBuddBillyBuddBillyBudd. "But being a rat is like me?"

"You had good reasons," said Dad. "And you weren't wrong."

Mike felt confused. What did Dad know? Was he talking to Cody? "I wasn't wrong about what?"

"You reported what you considered unlawful behavior." Smooth old Dad. Mike could imagine the anchor slipping off the boat into the water. Does the bullshit rise? "Misuse of school property—the computers—for what appeared to be unauthorized activities. Good for you. Turns out these were communication slipups, and I'm glad you brought them to the attention of people who can set things straight. Can we go to bed now?" He was smiling.

Mom said, "Scott?"

He sighed. "Yes, Sharon."

"Tell him."

"He's got enough on his mind."

"Scott." It was almost a bark. He'd forgotten how tough Mom could be.

"Now, Mike," said Dad, "we're going to work this all out."

"Work what out?"

Mom said, "Tell him or I will."

"Okay." Dad rubbed his hands together, the way he did when he was getting ready to make a sales pitch. Wait till you see this fabulous floor we've got for you. "So. Zack's mother is making a fuss. She's threatening to sue the school and us, says Zack has headaches and neck spasms since you pushed him. This was all in response to Mr. Cody shutting down the Cyber Club and suspending some of the members. They'll drop the suits if the club is reinstated.

"I worked out a plan with Mr. Cody to make this go away. He'll reinstate the club and the students if we help him out with a little immigration problem. Seems the Ramirezes are a tad short in the papers department. But if we establish an address for them here, at least Oscar will be eligible to attend Ridgedale and play ball."

"So Oscar and his dad are going to sleep here?"

"As far as people are concerned, yes," said Dad. "But not really. He left that bag here if anyone checks."

"So we're going to lie?" Mike's stomach hurt.

Mom came over and put a hand on the back of his neck. "This is just for a little while," she said. "It'll blow over. I know it's upsetting for you, but with the new store open-ing . . ." She kissed his cheek and hugged him.

"The new store." It just fell out of his mouth like a stone. "That's the only thing going on in the world."

He was about to apologize, but Dad raised his hand. "Let's not forget something, Mike. All this started when you slugged that little puke."

"Scott!"

Dad raised his arms, palms up. "Am I missing something here?"

"You're right, I started all this," said Mike. His mind was racing. Need to end this conversation right now.

"Look, Mike, there's a lot of things going on here." Dad dropped hand on his shoulder. "For now, just concentrate on playing the best center field you can. It'll all work out."

Somehow that made Mike feel better. It was a plan. "You can count on me."

"I knew that," said Dad.

He figured he'd never get to sleep tonight, so he logged on to the Buddsite. There was an alert. Billy has narrowed the candidates for his A Day With Billy contest to three—one each from New Jersey, New York, and Connecticut. All terrific, tough choice, results after the weekend series with Baltimore.

He tried to imagine a day with Billy. What would they talk about? Center field? Could he tell Billy about Oscar? No, that's stupid. He pushed Oscar out of his mind. The idea of Oscar even pretending to be next door in Scotty's room made him angry.

What was the deal with Coach Cody and Dad? Who was playing whom? Have to think that all through. Andy would be the one to talk to about that.

And Kat. She must have been driving. She thinks I'm a snitch. She hates me. That's why they doored me. So why did she call to see if I was okay? Does she know it wasn't me who told Cody? If I'm not the snitch, who is?

Mike was suddenly very tired. He logged off and fell into bed.

TWENTY-SEVEN

Oscar showed up for breakfast.

Mike was in the kitchen waiting for a ham-and-cheese sandwich to finish nuking when the old white van pulled into the driveway. He could see Ferdy through the windshield. Oscar climbed slowly out and stood in the driveway, arguing with his father. Ferdy reached through the passenger window and gave Oscar a shove. Oscar walked slowly toward the house.

"Scott," said Mom. She gestured out the window.

Dad opened the kitchen door. "Oscar! *Bienvenido!*"

Oscar looked reluctant, but entered after a moment.

Mom and Dad fussed over him, made him sit down. Mom said, "Have you had breakfast?" and when he nodded, head down, Dad said, "Can always have another one. Eggs, pancakes, French toast?"

Mom opened the cabinet where she kept more than

a dozen different kinds of cereals. Oscar's eyes widened. "Looks like a bodega," he said.

Even Mike laughed. Mom was big on breakfast and she was always finding new cereals to try.

Dad left for the store and Mom made Oscar pick a cereal. She loaded the bowl with blueberries, bananas, and milk. Oscar ate as if he were hungry. Mike felt a splash of jealousy. Mom hasn't made me a breakfast like that in years, he thought. He remembered that he'd been refusing cereal for years, didn't like it. Used to have fights over it. His ham-and-cheese breakfast sandwiches were a compromise; Mom made batches and froze them.

"'S good, thanks." Oscar had a big smile.

"Most important meal of the day," said Mom.

He needs his strength, Mike thought sourly, to beat me out of center field. Thanks, Mom.

Oscar didn't have anything to say on the ride to school. At the varsity parking lot, Oscar jumped out and walked away with a quick wave as if he didn't want to be seen with Mike. He headed toward the temporary trailers where the English as a Second Language classes were held. Mike had heard they were always either too hot or too cold.

Ryan fell into step with Mike as they walked up to the front door. "Keep your friends close and your enemies closer."

"He's on the team," said Mike. "He's no enemy."

"It's an expression," said Ryan. "From *Godfather II*."

Ryan slowed to talk to someone and Mike hurried through the door. He didn't want to talk to anyone about Oscar.

At lunch Andy said, "What's with you and Oscar?"

Ryan said, "Mike's coming out."

"That's not funny," said Lori.

"Maybe Mike's going to start smuggling illegals into New Jersey," said Andy. "Coyotes make much *dinero*."

"That's really not funny," said Tori.

"Oscar and his dad are staying with us for a little while," said Mike. The lie felt sour in his mouth. "It's the only way his dad can get to work on time."

"That is so nice," said Lori. Mike checked. No sarcasm there.

"Sounds to me you're establishing a false residence," said Andy.

"Sounds to me like you need to mind your own business," said Mike.

"As a citizen, it is my business," said Andy.

"As a friend," said Ryan, "you should just shut up."

"Was that the deal to get center field back?" said Andy.

"At least you lost first base to an American, right?" said

Mike. He was sorry as soon as he saw Andy's face flush a deep red, almost matching his hair. Maybe Andy really did care.

They ate in silence until the buzzer freed them.

Coach pulled him into his baseball office before the pre-game practice. "What's with Oscar and his dad?"

"They're fine."

"All squared away at your house?"

"They left some stuff last night and then came by this morning."

Coach nodded. "I like the way you've been handling yourself, Mike. Ranger steady. The team needed you in left field, you went there. You're back in center because you showed me grace under pressure."

"Everybody thinks I'm back because I ratted out Zack and the Cyber Club."

"Do they?" Coach was steering him out of the office. "Can't worry about what the pukes think."

"Why did you shut down the Cyber Club?"

"You just worry about center field, big fella, and you'll have a breakout day."

He did. First at bat, Mike lashed a double into the right-field hole and went to third on a botched relay. Oscar brought him home with a sacrifice fly. Two innings later

Mike hit his first homer of the season, with a man on.

There were no tough chances in center until the seventh inning, one out and the bases loaded, when Mike hit the fence making an over-the-shoulder catch. He bounced off, disoriented. Oscar, a foot away, yelled, "Secon' base," and Mike turned and fired blindly.

Todd cut off the throw in short center, spun, and threw to Hector, who doubled the runner at second base to end the inning.

Ridgedale won. Coach gave Mike the game ball. They yelled and sang in the bus all the way home. They were leading the conference.

There was no Herold in the phone book. He called information and checked it online. Nothing. He thought about calling Zack or Nick. Yeah, right. Then he remembered the Varsity yearbook. There it was, under Track. Katherine Anne Herold, 43 Harrison Road. Less than a mile away. He repeated her name as he rode, Katherine Anne, Katherine Anne. It rolled off his tongue.

The house was big, surrounded by an acre of lawn. Through the wide picture window he could see an old couple watching TV. No one else in the room. No lights in any of the upstairs rooms. Maybe she wasn't home yet. Catch her coming back. Hey, Kat, just happened to be out

for my evening ride. He circled the block and rode past
three more times. A man came out of the house next door
to play catch with his son and looked at Mike as if he was
a stalker. Maybe he was. He pedaled home.

TWENTY-EIGHT

Tori was breathless at lunch on Thursday. The Cyber Club kids were refusing to make a deal with the school. They were fighting their suspension. Lawyers were in the principal's office. She looked at Mike.

"They contact you yet?"

"Why should they? I didn't rat them out!"

"Like that's such a bad thing," said Tori, raising an eyebrow at him.

"Mike said he didn't and I believe him," said Lori. She sounded like she was being loyal.

He felt uncomfortable. He was relieved when the twins moved on to what Lori was going to wear to Craig's party tomorrow night.

He had another good game in center field. With Oscar in left, he could shade toward right field and help Ryan. Ryan caught anything he got to, but he didn't get to everything, he wasn't that fast. Oscar in left makes me a better center fielder, he thought. Don't have to think about left center. Or am I giving up territory that's mine?

Push that away, it's negative.

He was meeting the ball solidly, two hits today, one of them scoring a run. Another win. Oscar batting fourth makes me a better hitter because pitchers have to give me strikes, they can't afford to walk me with him coming up.

After the game he drove Oscar to the new store but Ferdy and his cousin had already left for their city job. They left word they would pick up Oscar on their way back to Orange County. Dad gave Mike money and told him to take Oscar to the diner.

They didn't have much to say. Mike had picked a corner booth where they would be out of sight. What am I doing with this guy? They both ordered the hamburger deluxe medium and Cokes. He noticed that Oscar ate very slowly, almost delicately. Mike was finished and Oscar was barely half done. He studied Oscar's face. Couldn't tell how old he was.

Back at the house Oscar dropped to his knees in front of the cat. She crawled right into his arms and purred. He was about to warn Oscar to watch out for her claws, but they were already nuzzling each other.

"You like cats?"

"Got three at home."

"At home?

"In the DR." When he saw Mike's puzzled expression, he said, "Dominican Republic."

"You miss home?"

Oscar nodded.

"You came here to play ball?"

He nodded again.

"Want to watch the game?"

Oscar picked up the cat. She burrowed into his neck.

Downstairs Oscar's eyes widened as the eighty-four-inch screen came down from the ceiling and the projector hummed to life. But he was too cool to say anything until a life-size Billy Budd swung two bats at them in the on-deck circle. Then he laughed. *Santa mierda.*

Mike got some Cokes and chips. "You like Billy?"

"The best, man."

"You got his stance."

"You, too." They clicked Coke cans.

Billy popped up to the shortstop. Oscar stamped his feet. "He need to wait for his pitch."

"He's batting .324."

"Should be more. Goes for too many bad balls."

"Did you go to one of those baseball academies in the DR?"

Oscar nodded. "Campo Juan Marichal. Oakland As."

"For how long?"

"Three years. Play every day."

"You signed with the As?"

He nodded.

"How come you're not playing pro ball?"

Oscar cracked his knuckles. Mike noticed how big his hands were. "You know what a *buscone* is?" When Mike shook his head, he said, "Like a scout. In the DR. When they sign you up with a team, they get some of your money. *Buscones* were ripping off kids and there was trouble. The Major League made the teams cancel some of the contracts."

"Yours?"

He nodded. "Don't know what's going to happen now." The long dark face looked miserable.

Mike felt badly for him. "What are you going to do?"

Oscar shook his head.

"How'd you come to Ridgedale?" When Oscar seemed to hesitate, he said, "I won't say anything."

"My uncle knew Hector's father and Hector told Coach about me. Coach said he could help get me papers. My dad, too."

"Is that happening?"

Oscar spread out his hands. The cat complained. "Don' know."

"You trust Coach Cody?"

Oscar shrugged. "Got to." He settled back into the couch.

The Yankee game was almost over when Oscar's cell rang. All he said was "Righ' there." He stood up, carefully put the cat on the couch, and shook Mike's hand. "Thanks, man."

Mike walked him to the front door. The van was waiting in the driveway.

He thought about Oscar. He didn't seem like a bad guy. Trying to survive. Probably should be playing center instead of me. Coach Cody put me back in center field because he's afraid I'll rat out Oscar. But he knows I didn't rat out the Cyber Club. I need to talk to Kat.

TWENTY-NINE

He had heard so much about Craig's parties that he was prepared to be disappointed, that it would turn out to be like all the other jock parties, just rowdier and boozier. He'd have a bigger headache than usual tomorrow. But the moment he and Lori walked through the door, he felt the difference. The air was damp with beer and sweat, and sweet with pot. The mood vibrated with gathering waves, like surf before a storm. It was pumping up to a wild night. Lori pressed against him. He thought she was thrilled and scared. He thought he might be, too.

"Here comes Mak, Mighty Mak," roared Craig. He had a bottle in his hand and he swayed. Wasted already. "Let's give it up for the man who busted the pukes."

Whistles and applause. Slaps on the back and butt. A glass was in Mike's hand. He was absorbed into a scrum of bodies. Lori was swept away by a couple of senior cheerleaders. A joint was pressed to his lips, he shook it away. Somebody laughed. He drank from the glass, nearly choked. It wasn't beer.

Mostly seniors, mostly jocks. Teammates appeared. He recognized a few guys he barely knew. Alumni. He'd heard that guys came home from college for Craig's parties. He saw Eric Nola's older brother, Derek, who had been team captain when Mike was a sophomore. He was playing at Montclair State now. He gave Mike a light shove to the chest with the heel of his hand. How I hit Zack, Mike thought. He wondered if that had been deliberate. Derek rocked back a step and shouted, "Mak the Man." He swayed away.

The music pounded through the house, the same music that came out of Craig's iPod dock in the locker room. Chief Loki was screaming, *"We own da season!"* until Strep started yelling, *"I'll tell you again I am unbreakable."*

He began to relax. Everybody was friendly. Everybody seemed to know him. Even the student government big shots. The tough kids he'd figured were the school's dope dealers all wanted to bump fists.

He felt drunk before he had had much to drink. His eyeballs were swimming in the glass bowl of his skull. Lori floated back into view. Was her makeup smeared or his sight blurry? She came into his arms. They danced.

He didn't know how long they had been there before

Craig pulled him away from Lori and whispered, "Follow me upstairs. Now."

Craig's girl had her arm around Lori and was leading her away.

The eight seniors on the baseball team were crowded into Craig's bedroom. They all had bats. He saw trophies jammed into bookcases and a huge poster of Roger Clemens on the wall. Even after the Rocket was busted he was Craig's hero. The lights went out. A single red bulb flicked on in a corner throwing a bloody wash across the sweating faces surrounding him.

The faces made a circle around him, started chanting, "Rangers, Rangers, Rangers."

A blindfold was tied around his head. His stomach churned. They were going to make him next year's captain.

DeVon's deep voice, "Who proposes?"

"I do." It sounded like Willie Lockett.

"Speak."

"He puts team ahead of himself. This is a stud who crashes into walls, who takes no shit, who can lead the Rangers."

"Who opposes?"

"I do." Sounded like Jimmy Russo.

"Speak."

"He's a coach's pet, never one of the guys," said Jimmy. "What made him change? What's his deal? Can he be trusted?" It sounded memorized to Mike. Was there a script?

"He bided his time," said Willie, "stepped up in the clutch."

"Nark's a nark," said Jimmy. "Weasels his way in. Drops the dime."

"Spies for the good," said Willie. "Like Nathan Hale."

"What say you, Captain?" said DeVon.

"Vote," said Todd.

One by one, eight voices said, "Yea!" Each banging his bat on the floor. Even Russo.

"So be it," said Todd. "Captain-elect Mike Semak. Do you accept?"

Before Mike could say anything, they were all on him, pummeling, poking him with their bats, pulling at his clothes. Someone had a hand between his legs. He fought his way free.

Jimmy Russo pulled him to his feet, whispered, "That was just part of the ritual, didn't mean it." He pulled off Mike's blindfold.

DeVon handed him a glass. "Drink the blood of the foe."

They all chanted, "Rangers, Rangers, Rangers," while he chugged it down. He had no idea what was in it besides alcohol that stung his nose and made his eyes water. He was dizzy. Who was the foe?

Downstairs there was more whistling and applause, more drinks. Lori hugged him. "I'm so proud of you, Mike."

He tried to say something and DeVon said, "Good thing he ain't captain of the drinking team."

Laughter in the fog.

He had no idea how he got home.

PART THREE

*"Yesterday's game is over and
tomorrow's game could be rained out.
Today's game is the only one on my mind."*
—IMs to a Young Baller by Billy Budd

THIRTY

He woke at noon with a weight on his chest. The moment he opened his eyes, the cat started meowing and digging her claws into his collarbone. She shrieked as he rolled her off. His mouth was dry. His head hurt. He was nauseous.

He was captain of the Ridgedale High baseball team.

It took more than an hour, a shower, tomato juice, coffee, and three ibuprofen tablets before he started to think clearly.

He was friggin' captain of the friggin' Ridgedale High baseball team!

He didn't bother checking his cell or computer—they would be packed with messages. Andy and Ryan would be coming over soon. Maybe even Lori. Mom and Dad would want to know. The day would disappear into the night and he'd never talk to the only person whose voice he wanted to hear.

If he was ever going to do it, he had to do it right now.

What if she's in a nasty Tigerbitch mood? Why wouldn't she be? She thinks you narked out the Cyber Club.

You gotta risk it. You can handle it. You're a jock.

Don't you remember that she said, I'm not into that these days?

Go for it, Captain Mak.

He called Kat.

"Hello." Her voice was clear, high.

"It's Mike."

"Mike." She sounded glad.

"Ready to run?"

"Now?"

"I'll come right over."

"You know where I live?"

He felt confident, strong, the Captain. "Forty-three Harrison."

"How do you know?"

"I'm a stalker."

She laughed. "Come around the back."

"See you in fifteen."

He was there in less than ten. He flew. He zoned into getting there fast. He didn't want to think about why her mood had changed. It had. Stay in the now.

He circled around to the back. It was one of those old mother-daughter houses. She had her own apartment with her own entrance. Peeking through a window, he saw her standing at a mirror, her T-shirt pulled up. She was pinching a roll of flesh at her waist and shaking her head. He had never thought of her as being at all self-conscious about her body. She was beautiful, an athlete in great shape, full of confidence. He felt a rush of warmth. He knocked on her door.

"That was fast."

"I ran."

She pushed up the bill of his baseball cap and looked into his eyes. "Rough night?"

"Sort of."

"How long you good for?"

"Try me."

She set a slow and steady pace until they reached the trails that wound through the county park and up into the hills. She picked it up. Her knee seemed fine. So was his ankle. They ran single file. She never looked over her shoulder to see his mouth open and gasping for air, the sweat pooled around his eyes. His legs felt heavy. Booze always goes to your legs. They were halfway up the first hill trail when she said, "You okay?"

"You?"

She lengthened her stride. He watched her long pale legs churn like pistons, the muscles bunching in her calves. The round cheeks of her firm, high butt rose and fell under her blue and gold running shorts. He wondered what they would feel like if he reached out and touched them. Sweat darkened her T-shirt between her shoulder blades. His own shirt was soaked. By the time they were at the top of the second hill he had lost any desire to touch her. He just wanted to keep up with her.

He spilled some water into his mouth and spit it out. Anything more on his stomach and he'd barf.

This is crazy, he thought. I'm a baseball player, not a runner. Drop back.

No way.

Tell her to slow down.

You kidding?

This some kind of macho thing?

Whatever.

He hurt all over. His hair hurt. His teeth ached. Billy said you have to know the difference between pain and injury. Pain is your body complaining. Maybe it's just tired, wants to quit. Injury is something wrong. You got to stop and take care of it.

He talked to himself. This is just pain, Mike. Hungover pain. Running faster than you're used to pain. Trying to impress a babe pain.

At least the ankle feels fine.

You can do it, Captain.

They reached the top of the last hill. He was pleased to see she was sweating and breathing hard, too. She bent over, hands on knees. She cocked her head at him. "Didn't think you'd make it."

He smiled at her. "Nothing better to do."

"I bet on you."

They laughed and sat down on the soft earth.

It was cooler up here. A light breeze tickled and chilled the drops of sweat. He used his cap to wipe his face and neck. They drank water and stretched out.

"So what was the occasion for getting wasted last night? Or don't you guys need one." She was gently teasing.

"How could you tell?" He rolled over on an elbow. She was on her back staring at the pale blue afternoon sky. Her hair was gathered under her baseball cap. Her neck was long and graceful. He wanted to touch it.

"Your eyes," she said. "They're always so clear, white and light brown. Today they're red-rimmed and a little muddy."

"I feel muddy," he said. "I was elected captain of the baseball team last night."

She sat up, smiled at him. "Congratulations."

He took a breath. Got to get it out in the open. "I'm captain because they think I ratted out the Cyber Club."

Her smile faded. "I know you didn't." She looked so intense, serious, he wanted to reach out and touch her face. "You couldn't have."

"You're the only one who doesn't think I did it. How come you're so sure?"

She hesitated. Watching her face, he thought she was about to say something, then swallowed those words and said something else. "You're a straight arrow."

He sat up and faced her. "Straight arrow? Is that like a dumb jock?"

"Straight arrow is honest, steady, dependable. Good."

Their knees almost touched. "Sounds boring."

"Doesn't have to be," she said.

They reached for each other at the same time.

THIRTY-ONE

The little apartment attached to the back of the house was neater than any of his friends' rooms, Mike realized, because there was was hardly anything in it. The pictures on the walls looked as if they had been bought by old people at a garage sale. Except for the purple laptop on an old rolltop desk and the red iPod in a dock on a nightstand alongside Kat's bed, there weren't too many clues that a high school kid lived here. None of the stuffed animals that gaped at you in Lori's room or the video games, dirty laundry, and sports equipment that littered the rooms that Andy and Ryan and he flopped in.

He looked at a tall black metal rack in one corner. He'd seen them before in a gym. You could hang upside down. "For your knee?"

"For my head," she said. "You hungry?"

Behind a set of folding doors was a tiny kitchen. Refrigerator, stove, sink, some cabinets with dishes. Without asking what he wanted, she started making sandwiches. He dropped into a black canvas sling chair. Hadn't seen one of these since his grandparents were alive.

"Who lives in this house?"

"My grandparents. My mom was raised in this house. *Her* grandparents lived in this apartment while she was growing up."

"Your folks split?" He didn't usually ask so many questions, he realized. He was hungry for information about her.

"It's more complicated than that." She seemed absorbed in slicing a tomato. "More than you want to know."

"Hey, straight arrows want to know everything." He thought he had said it comically but she turned sharply, her face tightening.

"Don't assume you own me because of what we did." The Tigerbitch voice was taking over, low, cold, sharp.

"I don't assume anything. I just like being with you." He realized he had never said that to Lori.

"What about your girlfriend. The twirler?"

"The one who deserves as much respect as the tubs of lard on the offensive line?"

Her face relaxed again. Her voice rose, warmed. "You my official biographer?"

"Job open?"

"Maybe." She handed him a plate with a sandwich. It was

turkey on whole wheat bread with lettuce and tomato. He bit in hungrily. "'S good, thanks."

She put a glass of orange juice on the floor next to his chair. He swallowed. "Pulp."

"More nutrients."

"That's what Mom says. Tastes like seaweed."

"That's good, too." She sat on her rolling desk chair and ate her sandwich. The music on her iPod speakers was familiar. Tiffany had blasted it constantly in her locked bedroom. Plenty of fights with Mom and Dad over that.

Kat caught him looking at the iPod. "Pink Floyd," she said as if he should know. *The Wall.*

Scotty hated it, called it music for crazy girls. Mike didn't want to think about that. He watched Kat eat from the corners of his eyes, the way he tracked a fly ball in the sun. She wasn't pretty and perfect like Lori, the nose and chin too sharp, eyes close together, but his breathing stopped when he looked at her, the strong teeth tearing off chunks of sandwich, the small muscles along her jaw pumping under the smooth skin. She closed her eyes when she swallowed.

He got excited remembering them holding each other on top of the hill. She had set the pace for their sweaty slick bodies. With Lori, sex was quicker, driving to climax. With Kat it seemed as if they were trying not to let it end. She seemed as sure of herself when she was making love as she did when she was running, older and more confident than she seemed now.

"Stop staring at me." Her voice was tense.

"Sorry." He looked down at his sandwich. "I can't help it."

"I'm so beautiful, right?" she said sarcastically.

He took a deep breath. "To me you are." Is that me talking?

She put the sandwich down and looked at him. He thought her eyes were gleaming. Tears? "You don't know anything about me."

"Enough," he said, "to know I care about you."

"Don't start caring too much." She looked away.

He felt she was slipping away from him. He thought about getting out of the chair, reaching for her, but he felt suddenly shy. Better wait for her to come back. At her pace. He realized he was afraid of her, at least afraid of upsetting her, changing her mood. He finished his sandwich and drained the orange juice. He leaned back in the chair, trying not to let his mind get lost in the music.

She finished her sandwich and turned toward him. Her eyes were dry. Steady.

"That rack?" She pointed at the black metal apparatus in the corner. "When I feel bad, I hang upside down like a bat."

"That works?"

"Most of the time. When it doesn't, I have pills. Running used to do it for me. It got really bad when I had to stop."

"You should come bike riding with me. That clears my head." As soon as he said it he was sorry because he knew where she would take it.

"Unless someone tries to knock you off. We were just going to talk to you." She looked down. "After he did it, I panicked and drove away."

"You don't panic."

"I'm always trying not to panic." She looked at him. "Sometimes I think I'm holding on by my fingers."

He struggled out of the sling chair and put his arms around her. "I can help you hold on."

She squeezed him tight. "What's going to happen now?"

"I don't know about tomorrow," he whispered into her ear, "but tonight's a movie night." After he said it, he thought it made sense. Something kind of normal.

"What?" She pulled back and looked at him with a comical expression. "Movie night?"

"We could go to a movie."

She smiled. "Like a date?"

"Straight arrows go on dates."

"You can be funny, you know that?" Her voice had perked up. She pointed at the laptop. "I usually watch movies on that. Or edit what I've been shooting."

"The Social Issues Project? Or the one you said you'll tell me about sometime?"

"The Billy Budd contest." She looked happy.

"What?"

"That little speech you made at the senior center about center field? I edited it with some shots of you and Billy in center field and sent it in."

"How could you do that?" He felt delighted and angry.

"It's easy with the software. . . ."

"Without telling me?" The anger faded at the look of hurt in her eyes.

"I thought you'd like it. Then with everything that happened I forgot about it. I guess you didn't win."

"Tomorrow night they announce the winner." He felt icy prickles down his spine. This is my week.

"Wouldn't that be something," she said. She wrapped her arms around him again. Something about the way she gripped him, he had the sense she was holding on.

When she released him, he said, "Show it to me."

She shook her head. Now she looked shy. "I don't want to jinx it."

"I'd like to see something you made."

She smiled at that. "What about movie night?"

"We'll have it here. We'll get a pizza."

She laughed. Her fingers started flying over the keyboard and the screen filled with faces.

THIRTY-TWO

In the dream Dad was shaking him awake Sunday morning, yelling, "How could you not tell us?" and Mike was struggling to remember what he hadn't told them.

No dream. Mom was right behind, smiling. "I'm so proud of you."

"This is terrific, really terrific, Mike," said Dad.

He remembered to cover himself before he sat up. "Terrific?"

"You kidding? Team captain? College sees that, you go to the top of the pile."

"Dinner tonight," said Mom. "I'm defrosting steaks."

"If you want to come to the store, we could use . . ."

"Homework," Mike said. "Getting behind, all the games."

"Sure."

He was disappointed at how easily Dad gave in. To the team captain.

Mom blew him a kiss at the door. "Breakfast's waiting for you. Gotta run."

Ryan walked in before he finished eating. "Yo, Captain Mak." Ryan poured himself a glass of orange juice, swallowed, and made a face. "Pulp."

"More nutrients. Seaweed's good for you, too."

"You're team captain, not team dietician." He looked around. "Nobody home?"

"I'm home, dipshit."

"Okay." Ryan lowered his voice. "It's none of my business. . . ." Ryan looked uncomfortable, his big open face twisted. Not like him, Mike thought, usually so direct. "Yeah, it's my business. You're my best friend. So. Guy in my fantasy league delivered an Everything Pie to Harrison Street and you came to the door and paid for it. Good tip. He saw a tall babe. Superbooty. I said, 'No way,' but he knows you."

"If it was a good tip it wasn't me." He looked away and kept eating.

"C'mon, Mike, I'm trying to be your friend here. The twins were already pissed you invited Zack and Tigerbitch to their party. I had to lie like crazy for you last night. We all were going to Nearmont and when nobody could find you I said there was some more captain stuff you had to do."

"Why'd you do that?"

"Cover your ass. Wouldn't you do that if I was slipping around on Tori?"

"Are you?"

He grinned. "I will if you'll cover my ass."

"You tell them?"

"It always gets around." The way he said it, Mike wondered if he had told Tori already. "What the hell are you doing? We've got a good thing going. How do you think you got home Friday night?"

He shrugged. He was tired of Ryan.

"Lori called Tori and me. We are your friends, man. Don't do this."

"You finished?"

"Over and out." Ryan slammed down the glass, stood up, glowered, then sat down and grinned. "So who was she?"

My best friend, thought Mike. I want to tell somebody. "Kat Herold."

"Yeah, right. C'mon, you can tell me."

"I just did."

Ryan blinked. "Tigerbitch?"

"I don't think . . ."

"I guess she was a pussy for you."

"We're done here," said Mike. Just like the defense lawyers said it on *Law & Order* when the interrogation of their clients got too hot. He stood up.

Ryan stood up just as quickly. "This is a big mistake."

"Go twirl."

Ryan was six-three, an inch taller and twenty pounds heavier, Mike thought, but I'm faster, probably stronger. Why am I processing this? He's my best friend. I haven't had a real fight with anybody since fifth grade. And I've never had a fight over a girl.

Ryan shrugged. "I'm not going to tell anybody. I've got your back, man. Like always." He walked to the door, turned, and said, "But it's a big fucking mistake."

Mike almost called out to him, to try to explain. He let him go. How could he explain what he didn't understand?

He shut off his cell and let the house phone ring. He barely moved for hours. Throughout the Yankee doubleheader, announcers teased the winner of the A Day With Billy contest. Stay tuned for the postgame show.

Once he would have creamed in his jeans thinking about the possibility of a day with Billy. Once? Just a little over three weeks ago. Not even a month since he pushed Zack. Now the best part of thinking about a day with Billy was that Kat had made the video. He felt warm and happy thinking about her. Yesterday was the best day of his life.

He'd enjoyed watching her short films. She was good.

Some of them were dazzlingly bright, skateboarders and old folks and computer geeks telling their stories over upbeat tunes. Others were dark, almost mysterious, shadows in graveyards and hospital corridors. He wondered how she felt when she shot each one, but he didn't ask. She showed him a rough edit of a series she was doing called A Year in the Life of Ridgedale High, a lot of quick cuts of kids and teachers in action, Dr. Ching at the laser board with a math problem, Coach Cody's hand signals, even Tori filing in the front office.

After they had watched for a while and eaten the pizza, he had reached for her. She pushed him away, shaking her head. "It's not like that."

"Like what?" He felt more confused than hurt.

"On demand. This afternoon was special. This would be just . . . routine."

There was something about that he could understand, even appreciate. When he kissed her cheek, she grabbed him and kissed his lips, hard.

He drifted in and out of the game. He had barely slept last night. He dozed through several at bats at a time. Billy was having an okay day, nothing special. Billy seemed to save his best days for the postseason, when it counted, when everybody was watching. The Yankees won the first game and were ahead in the second when Mom came home. He felt lonely and disconnected. When the cat ran upstairs sensing food, he trudged after her.

Mom was in the kitchen. "Dad'll be home soon." She peered at him. "Everything okay? Captain, sir."

"Just a little tired."

"When did you get home last night?"

"Really late."

"I thought the Burkises had a curfew during the girls' competition season." She laughed, then stopped as she looked at him. "You weren't out with Lori."

He wanted to talk about Kat. "Remember the varsity dinner last year? The girl who won the female sophomore of the year award?"

"Striking girl. Almost as tall as you."

"Her name's Katherine Herold. They call her Kat."

"Did you and Lori break up?"

Mistake. Would have done better emailing Catchergrrl or EmoBaller on the Buddsite than starting up with Mom. "No."

"Does she know about this?"

"Maybe."

"But not from you."

"No."

"You're my son, Mike, I'll always stand by you, but this isn't right. People deserve to know where they stand in a relationship. Are you going to break up with Lori?"

"I don't know what I'm going to do." He took a breath and thought *BillyBudd* three times. "But I know next time I'm not going to talk to you about it." He went back downstairs.

The second game was almost over. The Yankees were holding their lead. He waited until he heard his father's heavy steps in the kitchen before he came back up. He could tell they'd been talking.

Mom turned her back on Mike and Dad winked at him. "Mike's got to work this out for himself, Sharon. We can't meddle in his love life."

"It's not love life, Scott, it's life. It's about being a decent human being."

When the phone rang, Mom snatched it up. She said something sharp and hung up with a clack. "Don't you have your cell on, Mike? One of your friends."

"Who was it?"

"Who knows? Said he was calling for Billy Budd."

The phone rang again. Without thinking, Mike reached across her and picked it up. "Hello."

"Michael Semak? Ridgedale High School?"

"Yeah?"

"Dave Petry here. I work with Billy Budd. He wants you to come to the Stadium on Thursday, about noon."

It sounded like a joke but the voice was unfamiliar. All he could think of to say was, "I have school."

"I think they'll give you a day off for this. You've won the contest, Mike. A Day With Billy." He kept talking, but now it sounded like an echo from a distance.

Petry said that there would be another call from the Yankee public relations department and an email with instructions. He would be picked up at home on Thursday morning. He could bring one friend. Congratulations.

Mom and Dad were staring at him. He put down the receiver. "You're not going to believe this," he said.

THIRTY-THREE

Late Sunday night fielding messages from the Buddsite would have been more fun if he hadn't paused every few minutes to check for a sign of life from Kat. Nothing. Where was she? He imagined his voice mails, text messages, emails piling up in that neat little bedroom. He visualized running over to her house, sneaking around the back, tapping on her window. But something held him back. Afraid of Tigerbitch? Maybe.

The Buddsite was running Kat's video in a continuous loop. The Billybuds had plenty to say. EmoBaller sent a list of questions to ask Billy in person, mostly about shifting your weight in the batter's box. Catchergrrl wrote that Mike looked really cute on his winning video; he even looked a little like Billy. A couple of other girls linked to Facebook pictures of themselves.

He had hated the video the first time he saw his face filling the screen and heard himself babbling away "everything's there, spread out in front of you, and there's a right answer and a wrong one, but you have to figure it out. You can't fake it." Who is that jerk running his mouth?

The second time he watched it he began to relax. It wasn't that bad. "Center field is like being on top of the world seeing everything, spread out in front of you, coming at you."

It wasn't until the third viewing that he noticed that there were other people in the video besides himself, Zack and some of the other kids, old people from the senior center. The crazy old lady he'd been helping was smiling and nodding him on. Not so crazy. Entering the contest had been her idea. She had even coached him. He remembered she said, "Not so scrunchy," when he closed his eyes to visualize center field.

He thought, I had to watch this three times before I noticed anybody else in the video. Am I zoned in, or just a selfish, dumb jock?

The fourth time he began to appreciate what a terrific job Kat had done, smoothly intercutting all their faces with shots of Mike talking, shots of him and Billy in the outfield. Balls dropped out of the sky and into their gloves. "Just you and the ball." Kat had shaped it into something. She was talented. He'd like to tell her.

Where was she?

* * *

He heard a coughing muffler in the driveway. Oscar's back for breakfast, he thought. Must be coming back to school. Would Coach give Oscar center field back? Somehow, the thought didn't hurt like it used to. Got a lot of other things going.

But it was Hector standing in the kitchen, apologizing to Mom and Dad for disturbing them. Hector had never been in the house before. Mike had never had much to do with Hector.

Mom said, "Would you take Hector upstairs? He's come to get Oscar's things."

Hector grinned at the cello in a corner of Scotty's room. "You play that?"

"It's my brother's."

"I used to play. In middle school? The orchestra? Loved it, man."

He had never thought of Hector beyond second base. I don't really know anybody. "Where's Oscar?"

"Had to leave town." Hector seemed to know what he was looking for. He picked up Oscar's little blue duffel bag where Mike had dropped it at the foot of the bed.

"Is he coming back?"

Hector shrugged.

"C'mon, man, what's going on?"

Hector held up his hands. "He got screwed up, okay?"

"I know that, the *buscones* ripped him off. . . ."

"How you know that?" Hector squinted up at him.

"He told me. The contract stuff. Your dad, his uncle. Coming here to try to hook on with another pro team."

Hector nodded. "Yeah. He liked you. Said you had game. He tell you about Coach?"

"He said Coach was taking care of his papers."

"Yeah, he took care of it." Hector made a sour face. "Left him on base, man, just left him hanging."

"What do you mean?"

"When the Immigration started nosing around, Coach said Oscar had lied to him, gave him a phony birth certificate and a false address. Like he didn't know Oscar was twenty and lived in New York."

Mike's stomach turned over. "What are we going to do?"

"Play ball, man. What else?" Hector hoisted the duffel bag and went downstairs.

Walking into school, he felt different, as if he had come back changed from a great adventure. But everything else seemed the same. Biggest weekend of my life, he thought, Captain, Kat, Billy, life-altering events. He was pleased and uneasy when Coach Cody pulled him out of homeroom and led him to his office. Pleased that at least somebody acknowledges that something happened. Uneasy because he wanted to ask Coach about Oscar and about the Cyber Club.

Coach closed the door behind them. He sat behind his desk, let Mike stand. "Been thinking about what it means to be captain?"

"A little."

"You've got two main jobs. Number one is to act as liaison between me and the team. You let me know what the team is thinking, especially what they don't want me to know, so I can make good decisions for them. You tracking?"

He nodded. Now he wants me to nark on the team. Be his mole. Nothing changes.

"Number two is to lead by example. You don't need to make speeches. You have to show everybody how to give their all, to put the team ahead of themselves. It's about work ethic and stepping up when the road gets rocky. You can do that. I think you're capable of becoming a great captain."

"I'll try." He felt disappointed. That's all?

"I'm counting on it. It's why I picked you. Any questions?"

Why I picked you? I thought the seniors on the team picked me.

"What's with Oscar?"

Coach Cody sighed, took off his Ridgedale cap, and

rubbed a hand over his scalp. There was a scratchy sound. Mike noticed the coach's head wasn't as smooth and shiny as usual. Didn't shave it today. He looked tired around the eyes.

"Kid's caught up in some nasty business. I don't know if I can help him."

"Because he's illegal?" said Mike.

Coach said, "Oscar was a hot prospect a couple of years ago in the Dominican Republic and he signed with a Major League team. The local Dominican scout who signed him took most of the bonus money. The club knew about it, but that's the way the Major League teams do business down there. Instead of paying the scout themselves, they look the other way when they steal money from the boys.

"Well, there's been an investigation and it looks bad for the clubs. So they've cut their ties with some of the boys to avoid further investigation. Oscar got caught in that mess. His contract was canceled."

Same story that Oscar told. Probably true. But there's more. "Is Oscar illegal?"

"Talk to your dad about that," said Coach. "He can set you straight on the way of the world."

Mike felt a flash of anger. "What does that mean?"

Coach didn't look at him. "One more thing, Mike. Zack and that bunch are back in school. The district wimped out.

Afraid to stand and fight. But we don't have to welcome them back with open arms. The Cyber Club is done, but they still have no place here. You tracking me?"

If he didn't track Coach's words, he could track the hard glint in his eyes, the tight smile. All he could do was nod. He was wimping out and the anger turned sour in his stomach.

Coach stood up. "You're going to be a great captain, Mike." He reached across the desk to shake his hand.

THIRTY-FOUR

Lunch started out easier than he expected. Lori forgave him for standing her up Saturday night. She assumed he had still been wasted from Friday night at Craig's. She giggled and said she had never seen him so ripped. Some part of him wanted to tell her about Kat, some part was terrified she would find out. Or worse, Tori would find out. Ryan avoided looking directly at Mike.

They talked about the day with Billy. A cheerleader's boyfriend had heard the announcement after yesterday's doubleheader and word had whipped around. But nobody asked Mike who he was going to take. He figured both Ryan and Lori thought they were in the running. They would have been a few days ago. A tough choice then. But there was only one person he wanted to be with now.

"So who shot the video and sent it in to Billy?" asked Lori.

Mike was still figuring out an answer when Andy gestured across the cafeteria and said, "Look. Return of the computer virus."

Zack was settling down at the geek table. Fatty, Skinny, and the Chinese kid were there. The girl with the Mohawk. He searched for Kat. He had an urge to go over and ask about her.

"They cut a deal over the weekend," said Tori. "The Cyber Club is history. No lawsuits. No permanent records."

"Predictable," said Andy. "Left-wing pukes always get a pass."

"How is that a pass?" said Lori. "They shut down the Cyber Club."

"They should be expelled," said Andy.

"Hey, look," said Ryan. "There goes Rappy."

The big sophomore first baseman, Mark Rapp, was swaggering around the geek table, flipping trash off their trays onto their laps. Craig must have sent Rappy out. It was too far away to hear what he was saying to the geeks, but they were getting upset. Fatty tried to stand and Rappy pushed him back down into his seat. Craig and Eric Nola had strolled up and were laughing him on.

"That's not right," said Lori.

"It's not right they're back in school," said Tori.

The twins glared at each other.

Mike didn't realize he was on his feet until he heard

ROBERT LIPSYTE   221

Mike didn't realize he was on his feet until he heard
Ryan say, "Where you going?" It sounded more like a warning than a question.

He heard silverware clatter on the floor. You never hear that in the noisy cafeteria, he thought. The big room was falling silent. As he got closer, he could hear Rappy.

"You pukes got no shame. Nobody wants you here. Go to some gay school."

"Yo, Captain Mak." Craig was grinning at him. "Should we trash can 'em?"

"Leave them alone," said Mike. His voice boomed in the hushed room.

"Whose side you on?" said Eric.

Mike pushed Rappy away from the table. The big sophomore didn't resist. He looked confused. "Wassup, Cap?"

"Hey, Semak." DeVon had sauntered up. "Mind your business."

"We're supposed to set an example," said Mike. He wondered where that was coming from. Coach Cody? Billy Budd?

Zack stood up. "We can take care of ourselves, Semak."

DeVon and Nola snickered. Mike spotted Coach Cody standing in a corner of the cafeteria, arms crossed. No expression on his face. But we don't have to welcome them back with open arms. He must have said that to Craig, too.

"We're jocks, not bullies." Definitely Billy. He stood between the geeks and his teammates. He noticed Craig's eyes flick over his shoulder. He turned and saw a flash of red hair. Andy was behind him. Ryan must be there, too. He felt a surge of love for them. They had his back.

"You're not captain yet," said Craig. His face was getting red. Watch out.

So what would Billy Budd do?

The geeks were frozen, Zack the only one standing. He's figuring out it's not about him anymore, Mike thought. Craig, DeVon, Eric, and Rappy were watching him like wolves trying to figure out if they should attack or not. Nobody else on the team had come over. The on-field team leaders, Todd and Jimmy Russo, were sitting this one out. Coach Cody hadn't moved.

It's your play, Mighty Mak.

He tried to remember a story he had read about Billy defusing a situation in the Yankee clubhouse. Dwayne Higgins was involved. A new player had made a racial slur. A couple of other Yankees joined in and there was some pushing and shoving until Billy moved in and quieted them down. What had he said?

"C'mon, we're Rangers, we don't need to do this. We show everybody what we're made of on the field. These guys"—he gestured at the geek table—"go to this school so we represent them, too. We're supposed to be their role models. Show them how to act."

Eric and DeVon looked down and Rappy looked at Craig, the only one who kept glaring at Mike. I got them, thought Mike. Let it sink in. Don't go too far. Don't let this turn into a fight.

"You heard him," snarled Andy. "Take a hike."

Mike whirled. "Shut up, Andy."

Andy was standing alone. Ryan wasn't there.

"We've made our point—let's go," said DeVon. He turned and swaggered off. Eric followed him, then Rappy, glancing over his shoulder at Craig.

Craig said, "You watch your ass, Semak."

"You watch yours, asshole," growled Andy.

Craig lunged, but Mike got between them and pushed Andy away. He didn't look over his shoulder, just pushed Andy all the way back to their table. Kids were applauding and whistling.

Lori's eyes were shining. "That was wonderful, Mike."

Tori said, "That was stupid."

Mike looked at Ryan.

Ryan looked at Tori.

"You don't think I was going to let him get in the middle of that?" said Tori.

"Didn't need him," said Andy. "The Captain and I handled it."

Mike noticed that Coach Cody was gone.

THIRTY-FIVE

Get into the zone. Prepare for Billy. He was deep in the Buddsite, roaming between the Billyblog and the Billy Boards looking for topics to talk to Billy about. He found stories about how Billy's dad, Big Bill, coached his Little League teams and never missed a high school or community college game. Mike wondered if Big Bill knew Coach Cody. He wondered if that story was true.

Mike was less interested in the stories about Billy's girl-friend decorating their new house but he skimmed through them. Billy had adjusted his swing in spring training and was trying out a lighter bat this year. I could ask him about that. And about how he and Dwayne talked over how to play opposing hitters.

Catchergrrl wanted to know who he was going to take to the Stadium. Thanks for breaking the zone. The only person I want to take isn't answering me. I'll give her until the last minute. And then I'll go alone. Who else? Ryan? Not after today at lunch. Andy would say something stupid. Lori. How could he take Lori when he was thinking about Kat?

Back to the Buddsite. There were posts about the Billy Budd Foundation and how much time he spent visiting sick kids. Mike even found a mention of one Mike Semak, the star center fielder from Ridgedale (NJ) High who had won the video contest. "Star." I wish. He heard a distant knocking sound. The audio system again, he thought. He ignored it.

It took him awhile to realize the knocking was Mom's light but insistent rap on his bedroom door. "Yeah?"

She came in with her lips pursed and her eyes narrowed. "You have a visitor."

Was it Kat? He had to restrain himself from pushing past her to run downstairs.

It was Zack, sitting in the living room making awkward conversation with Dad. Zack sat perched on the edge of the couch, clutching his black bag to his chest. He looked ready to run away.

"Look who's here, Mike," said Dad, as if he were introducing Billy Budd.

"Hey," said Mike.

Zack stood up. "I need to talk to you?"

"Sure. Come on up." He noticed the look of disappointment on his parents' faces and the relief on Zack's.

Zack followed him into his bedroom, blinking at all the Billys on the wall. "He plays for the Yankees, right?"

For an instant Mike thought it was geek humor. The guy was serious. He's in his own league.

"Mike, um, thanks for, um, stepping up. In the cafeteria?"

"I did it for the planet." When Zack didn't react, he added, "I knew you could take care of yourself."

Zack nodded. "That was dumb. Josh and Tyler busted me on that."

Josh and Tyler must be Fatty and Skinny, Mike thought. Figured they had names.

Zack opened his black case and carefully withdrew a video camera. "Kat thought you might want to take it to the Stadium."

"You saw her?"

"She came back to get some clothes. She was just here for a little while. She said she'd call you. Sometime."

"Sometime?" It didn't sound like his voice. Whiny.

"She, um, she's not in a good place."

"Not in good place?" He felt angry and impatient. "Afghanistan? Darfur?"

Zack looked at him as if he were surprised Mike had

heard of those places. Then he threw up his hands. "She'll tell you."

"Sometime."

"She was happy you won. She wants you to take pictures. I'll show you how. We can email them to her."

"She doesn't answer my emails."

Zack looked unhappy. "She really likes you. She told me."

"And she won't answer me?"

"She gets weirded out sometimes. Feels bad. She calls it going dark."

"Like depressed?"

Zack nodded.

"Where is she?"

Zack kept nodding. Mike thought of a toy he had as a kid, a wooden bird that kept dipping its beak in water. Mike wanted to grab his head.

He took a deep breath. *BillyBuddBillyBuddBillyBudd.* "What's going on? Is she like having a breakdown?"

"I'm not supposed to . . ."

"Look, you can tell me. I really like Kat. I care about her."

Finally Zack said, "I don't know that much. A couple of years ago she had problems with her mother's boyfriend. Some stuff happened. She came here to her grandparents. And then . . ." He threw up his long flappy arms.

"Then what?"

"She was doing fine. Loved to run. Hurting her leg was a bummer. Track coach said it was all in her head because he wanted her to race. Then it got worse and Kat had to stop running. Then she started coming to the Cyber Club, but Cody heard about it and gave her a hard time. That's when she ripped the word Rangers off her uniforms. He threatened to throw her off the team if she didn't nark on us. Threatened to reveal her psychiatric record when she applied to college."

"Isn't that illegal?" said Mike.

"Yeah, but he would do it."

He thought of Cody putting pressure on Kat to nark. Unlike me, she refused. I've got to see her, at least talk to her.

"She told Cody to stick it, didn't she?" said Mike.

"Yeah, but he confiscated the video she shot at the conference. What he wants is on that tape, me running my mouth."

"About hacking Cody?"

Zack shook his head. "I kind of lost it there, trying to get everybody wound up. I'm the one to blame. And Kat's beating herself up for not destroying the tape. But how would she know?"

"Where is she?"

"It's like a group home. She's been there before."

He remembered what Lori had said. "Is she, uh, bipolar?"

"You some kind of shrink?" said Zack sharply.

"I really want to talk to her," said Mike softly.

"She has good days and bad days. She takes meds. Give her a little time."

"I thought maybe she'd come with me on Thursday."

"She would if she could, believe me." He looked at his watch. "I gotta book. Let me show you how to use the camera."

"You know how?"

"Well, obviously," the smart-ass Zack snapped back. Can't help himself. Social skills.

But the puke is my only way to find Kat again, thought Mike. He had a crazy idea. "How'd you like to come to Yankee Stadium with me Thursday?"

THIRTY-SIX

Billy Budd sent a limo.

Zack was waiting with Mike at the end of the driveway when the long black car glided up. Zack gawked until Mike elbowed him. "Start shooting." He imagined Kat would get a kick out of this.

Zack dug the camera out of his bag. He got the driver jumping out to open a back door, and Mike grinning and waving at his parents as he climbed in.

They didn't say much on the ride down the Palisades Parkway, the Hudson River gleaming on their left, over the George Washington Bridge, and into the Bronx. Zack mumbled something about poor people being uprooted to make way for the new Yankee Stadium, but Mike barely heard him. He was concentrating on not worrying about trying to make conversation with Billy Budd because it gave him a stomachache. What do you say to a god?

An advertising billboard with the date—Thursday, April 24—reminded him that it was exactly five weeks since he had shoved Zack. I should tell him it's our anniversary, he thought. But the guy has no sense of humor. Some anniversary. Shoving Zack was the worst thing I've ever done and look how great it turned out; I'm the starting varsity center fielder in the middle of a great season, captain-elect, met a great girl, and I'm on my way to meet my all-time hero.

The limo pulled up at the glass doors of the Yankee Stadium office entrance. The driver jumped out to open their door. A chunky young guy in a wrinkled white shirt and a loosened tie rushed out to meet them.

"Mike," he said, sticking a hand out. "Dave Petry. Let's go. Billy's waiting for you." He ignored Zack and led the way into the Stadium. He walked fast.

Security guards waved them through doors into a concrete corridor circling the Stadium, then into a dark tunnel that poured them out into an explosion of dazzling sunshine, green grass, blue sky.

From the right field foul line, the Stadium was immense, the grandstands rising like cliffs. As they walked onto the field, the Stadium grew around them, higher, wider, until Mike felt as though he were at the bottom of a canyon. He had seen games from seats all over the park but never before had any idea of the hugeness of the field, the height of the stands, the vastness of the sky with the sun as spotlight.

He tried to imagine the thrill and the pressure of playing here, of what it must be like to be Billy in the center of the universe.

"Let's go." Dave Petry was pulling him toward the Yankee dugout.

Billy Budd was bigger than Mike had imagined, taller and broader. Mike had to consciously slow his breathing. Billy was listed at 6-3, 220 pounds, but most of the time, Mike knew, the ball clubs added inches and pounds to their stars' statistics. Billy was as big as advertised. He wore a fresh white pin-striped home uniform, without a cap. His short brown hair glistened.

His spikes clacked on the dugout steps as he climbed up.

Billy glowed. His big white smile welcomed them. "Hey, young baller. Congratulations. Great video."

He stuck out his hand to Zack, who jumped back.

"This is Mike," said Dave, guiding Billy's outstretched hand away from Zack. "Billy hasn't had a chance to study the video carefully."

"Yo, Mike," said Billy. His hand was huge, callused.

His eyes, thought Mike, didn't seem as shiningly alive as the rest of him. They were clear and brown, but they were on guard. They checked out Mike, roved over his shoulder at the players on the field, then up to the early crowd, warily, as if he were checking for snipers.

"Hi, Billy." Mike's throat, dry, closed up.

"Photo op," said Dave. He pushed Mike and Billy together. Several photographers hurried up, posed them. Zack was shooting, too.

Side by side Mike realized that Billy wasn't that much bigger than he was. An inch or so taller maybe, at least twenty pounds heavier, but Mike didn't feel small next to him.

After a few minutes Billy said, "Gotta get my BP." He clapped Mike on the shoulder and ran back to the dugout to get a bat.

"BP?" said Zack. "They take blood pressure before a game?"

"You're kidding, right?" When he saw the blank look on Zack's face, Mike said, "Batting practice."

"Great guy, huh?" said Dave. They watched Billy run into the batting cage and take his swings, then grab his glove and run out into center field.

Mike and Zack trailed Dave as he pointed out Yankees. He introduced Mike to Dwayne Higgins, who shook his hand, then spat sunflower seeds on his shoes and cackled. "Next year, dude, you win a Day with Dwayne and have some fun." He winked and went to the bat rack.

They went down into the dugout, through another tunnel, and into the clubhouse. Mike shook hands with a young guy carrying towels who gave them a tour of the lockers, fancy cubicles with CD players and hair dryers. Billy had two lockers with a high director's chair in front of them. There was a sign on the chair—Captain.

It was dreamlike yet creepy. He thought he should feel thrilled, at least pumped, but he didn't feel much of anything. He pushed himself back into the now.

Dave hustled them into an elevator that opened onto a corridor high over home plate and into a wood-paneled room whose walls were filled with pictures of great old-time Yankees, Babe Ruth and Lou Gehrig, Joe DiMaggio, Mickey Mantle, Yogi Berra, Reggie Jackson. Mike could tell Zack didn't really know who most of them were.

They were served cafeteria-style, overcooked burgers and coleslaw, and sat down at a table. Dave brought a few reporters over, rumpled mumbly guys and fast-talking young women who asked a few questions about where Mike went to school.

One of them said, "What do you think of all this?"

"'S great," said Mike, his mouth full.

Dave was tapping into his handheld. "Highlights so far?"

Zack said, "Billy thinking I was Mike."

"Let's delete that," said Dave. "Other highlights?"

"What's this for?" said Zack.

"The Billyblog."

"You write that?" said Mike.

"A couple of us, yeah, after we talk it over with Billy."

Zack looked at Mike. "You thought Billy Budd wrote it?"

"Nearly forgot," said Dave, reaching into a black plastic garbage bag. He pulled out caps and T-shirts and a Yankee jersey with Budd across the back. They were all autographed by Billy. "For you guys."

They watched the game from a cramped corner of a radio broadcast booth. At least Mike did. Dave was writing on his computer and Zack was texting. Mike wondered if Kat was on the other end. He thought about sending something to Mom and Dad. They'd be busy at the store, but they had been excited about him going to the Stadium. Now they were excited because Scotty was coming home for a day on his way to Europe to play in a chamber music competition. Tiffany might be able to come home to see him.

From high up behind home plate, the entire field was spread out in front of him. He concentrated on watching Billy, the way he shifted position for different hitters and called out to the other outfielders. Billy was never quite still in the field, pounding his glove, transferring his weight from foot to foot, checking the flags in the outfield to see which way the wind was blowing. He was totally in the game, every moment.

In the seventh inning, Billy went all out for a long fly.

He caught it at the warning track, but limped back to the dugout.

"That quadriceps again," said Dave.

When Billy didn't go into the field for the eighth, Dave made a call on his cell. "Billy's going to the hospital now, check out that quad. Afraid we won't get to talk to him."

After the game they followed Dave back down to the corridor past the clubhouse. Mike spotted Billy first, his arm across the shoulders of a pretty blonde who looked like the model on the Buddsite. Dave looked uncomfortable. Had he been caught in a lie, Mike wondered, or had he gotten the wrong information? Billy pointed at Mike and motioned him over.

"The kid who won my contest," said Billy.

The blonde smiled. "Congratulations." She was shaking Mike's hand when her eyes flicked over Mike's shoulder. "Billy, is that the girl we met from *American Idol*?" She dropped Mike's hand to wave.

Dave walked them outside. The limo was waiting.

"I might call you later or email," said Dave. "For more of your reactions."

"Just make it up," said Mike. "Like usual."

Zack laughed. Well, that's something, Mike thought.

THIRTY-SEVEN

He felt sad. He watched the late afternoon sun sparkle on the Hudson River as the limo cruised up the parkway. Zack was quiet for most of the ride, his face close to the camera. He was viewing the video he had shot.

After a while Zack said, "Seems like a nice enough guy."

"What?"

"Billy Budd."

"He was okay."

Zack put the camera in his lap. "What'd you expect?"

Mike thought about that. His mind felt numb. "I don't know."

"You sound disappointed."

Mike looked at Zack. He had such a long, serious face. "Kind of."

"He was your hero, right?"

Mike nodded. It seemed childish now.

"I met my hero once. Ralph Nader."

Mike knew the name from Social Issues. "He ran for president, right? Pissed people off because he took votes away from their guy."

"Yeah. But before that he was really out there, going up against big business, starting grassroots consumer organizations. The bad guys went after him, but he was tough. Never gave up."

"You met him?"

"Yeah. He was okay. Brushed off my question. I guess it wasn't as good as I thought. He was busy."

"You were disappointed?" said Mike.

"Yeah. My mom said I should concentrate on remembering why I admired him. The guy had a real impact on America."

Mike felt a little flush of affection for Zack. Guy was trying to make him feel better. And he was.

And then he spoiled it.

"Of course, Billy Budd's just a jock."

"Dumb jock, you mean?"

Zack looked sorry. Maybe he just can't help himself. "I didn't mean that."

"Sure you did," said Mike. "You've said it before."

Zack chewed on his lower lip as if he were chewing

on a thought. "I was having a real bad day. When you pushed me?"

"I thought I slugged you. Gave you headaches and post-traumatic stress."

"That was our lawyers. When the school was trying to expel us."

"For hacking into school files?"

"I told you we never did it."

"Just talked about it," said Mike. Like a puke. And messed up Kat. Give him a break. "So what was your bad day? When I . . . pushed you."

"We had just found out Mr. Cody had canceled funding for the Cyber Club after the school board okayed it."

"How could he do that?"

"At Ridgedale he can do whatever he wants."

"That's what Andy says."

"Even a stopped clock is right twice a day."

Mike remembered that Kat had said that. Mike laughed. There was something honest and solid about Zack. He might be a puke with no social skills, but he didn't pretend to be anything else. Honest in his way. Took the blame for shooting off his mouth. He couldn't remember the last time he had talked with a guy when it wasn't about sports or girls. "I was having a bad day, too. I just found out a new kid was set to play center field."

"Oscar Ramirez."

"You know him?"

"He was at the district office when we were there. I think they're going to deport him."

"Is he illegal?"

"Cody said so. Said Oscar and his dad had lied to him about their status and given him a phony birth certificate. He was angry at them for pretending they were living in the school district. Told us that anyone who crosses him can expect no mercy."

"Did he say how he found out Oscar lied to him?"

"He said he was suspicious and checked him out."

They rode in silence for a while. Mike's head hurt from trying to follow Cody's lies. Finally he said, "So how come you never hacked in?"

"Now I'm sorry I didn't. Kat needed to know what was in her school record. Cody's such a liar, he could have been bluffing. Maybe there wasn't anything there."

"So who was the mole?"

"Nick," said Zack. "He showed up at the district office and you could tell which side he was on. And he knew Kat was shooting video while I was talking. She felt so bad. That's why she split."

Mike felt a lead weight in his stomach. Poor Kat. That bald-headed asshole really knows how to twist people up. He wanted to hold her, tell her it was all right.

"Ranger psych," said Mike.

"What's Ranger psych?"

"Psychological warfare. What Cody learned in the Army Rangers."

"He was in the Navy," said Zack. "The SEALS."

"Where'd you hear that?"

"He told us at one of the meetings. Show how tough he was. One of our lawyers had been in the Rangers, and when Cody heard that he said he was in the SEALS."

"That makes no sense. He changed the team names to Rangers, he talked about the Rangers all the time."

"A lot of different stories going around," said Zack. "Like your dad gave Oscar's father a job so Cody wouldn't suspend you."

Mike thought about it. "That could be true. He came back that day and said he'd worked out some kind of deal."

"Did your dad know they were illegal?"

"He got mad when I asked him. Said they worked hard and showed up."

"He got that right."

The numbness in his mind was gone, but he had a headache. Too much information. "So what are you going to do now?"

"What do you mean?"

"All your projects. The senior center. On-High dot org."

Zack shrugged. "Everything's on pause. We're all on

probation. We have to report to Cody once a week. Tell him what we've been doing."

"You can tell him about Billy Budd. What a dumb jock he is."

That got a smile out of Zack. "Yeah, right. He's gonna be on you for taking me."

"We can take care of ourselves." He tried to mock the high whiny voice Zack had used in the cafeteria.

"I meant that," said Zack. "Where did you come off saying you were supposed to be our role models, show us how to act?"

"You didn't like that?"

"Would you?"

"When are pukes role models?"

"Pukes?"

"Sorry. It's a word we . . ."

"Like dumb jocks?" said Zack.

Mike laughed. "I'm not as dumb as I look."

"How could you be as dumb as you look?" said Zack.

Mike threw a long, soft jab slow enough that even Zack could duck it.

"I think you just made your first joke," said Mike.

They both laughed the rest of the way home. The limo dropped Zack off first. Mike sensed that Zack was also trying to come up with something more to say, but they just nodded good-bye.

THIRTY-EIGHT

Coach Cody ambushed him. He strode out of his office as Mike walked into school Friday morning. He must have been watching the front door. Mike tensed.

But Coach was smiling. "Mighty Mak! Got a minute?"

Could he say no? He followed Cody back into his office. Muscles rippled under his tight white shirt. His head was freshly shaved. Smelled of cologne.

Coach gestured Mike to a chair and perched on a corner of his desk. The friendly position. "Talk to me about Billy Budd. What's he like?"

"He was nice. Was he a nice kid in Little League?"

Coach waved the question away as if he were sorry he had ever mentioned it. "Zack enjoy himself?" The Coach's smile seemed frozen.

"I guess so." He felt a need to fill the silence. "He'd never been to a ball game before." He was sorry he said that.

Didn't need to. Was Cody's silence part of Ranger psych? SEAL psych?

"How come you took Zack?"

"My dad wanted me to," said Mike. Lying exhilarated him. He was in the zone. Maybe I can play this game. Cody thinks I'm a dumb jock. "He's still afraid they'll sue us for hitting him."

Coach's eyes narrowed. Was he buying this? Did it matter? Am I keeping him off balance? "That makes sense." He slid off the desk and stuck out his hand. Mike stood up and shook it. "I like the way you're handling this, Mike. I've always had the feeling you were a leader. See you at the game."

His mind was a sandstorm all morning. What am I doing? What's my plan? I can just cool it now, play center field, stay out of trouble. Oscar's gone, Kat's gone, everything's back to normal, where it was five weeks ago before I shoved Zack. But I'm different.

Dr. Ching came up with a new problem. A pilot is performing loop-de-loops when his plane abruptly disintegrates. What happens to the pilot? Does he plummet straight down or spin off into space or continue the loop-de-loops? I am the pilot, he thought. Everything is coming apart. Will I fall, spin off, or continue in the same old patterns? Do I have a choice?

In math at least there will be an answer.

In Social Issues Andy seemed to have lost some of his steam without Kat. I know how he feels.

And then lunch.

Lori, Tori, and Ryan were careful not to look at him as he approached their table. Andy was across the room striking out with a girl at the Young Republicans table. Got to talk to Andy about his approach. Like I'm such a role model.

He briefly considered sitting down at the geek table. Zack looked up and nodded but was too cool to call out or wave. Mike was grateful for that.

Not a good time to appear too friendly with Zack, he thought. Bite the bullet.

He sat down next to Lori. Her eyes were red-rimmed.

"How could you?" she said.

"Because he's a . . ." said Tori. She couldn't or wouldn't find the word.

It took him a moment to figure out what they were talking about. By that time Tori had her arm around Lori and was pulling her out of her chair and away from the table. Mike looked at Ryan, who was studying his cheeseburger as if it were a lab specimen. "Thanks. Brah."

Ryan shrugged. "They were bound to find out, hoss."

"From you?"

"Tori knew something was going on. She asked me point-blank. Can't lie to her."

"Like you can't back me up if she tells you not to."

Ryan's face hardened. He'd never seen him angry before. "You screwed things up, man. You forgot who your friends were. We had a good thing going."

"You had a good thing going. Because you're just a dumb jock."

Mike kicked his chair back as he stood up and stomped out of the cafeteria. He kept going out to the parking lot.

It was the first time he'd ever walked out in the middle of a school day without a pass. It was an outlaw feeling that scared and excited him. The same way being with Kat scared and excited him. He thought about her as he drove to the county park and walked alongside a slow shallow river. He followed the river path toward hills that looked like steps up to the early afternoon sun. He remembered running the hill trails with Kat and then making love on the soft earth of the top. Slow and gentle at first and then rougher. He felt freer than he did with Lori, not afraid of hurting her. She wasn't as heavy as he was but almost as long and very strong.

But in some ways she wasn't strong at all. And now she's gone.

So what are you going to do now, Mighty Mak? Send another question to the Buddsite? What did you expect from Billy? Jesus in a Yankees cap? Coach let you down. Ryan let you down. Dad let you down.

You are really out there, man, all by yourself, racing the ball to the wall, and this time the ball is your life and if you miss it, if it goes over your head, if you turn the wrong way when you hit the fence . . .

Think positive. You'll catch it, make the throw home. He looked at his watch. Time to go back and make the game. Cody might know you ditched, but he won't do anything. He wants to win.

He felt loose and strong, in a sweet, mindless zone where nothing existed except the ball coming at him. Coming TO him. He could make out the seams, read the lettering, track the spin, see the moment his bat made contact, crushing the roundness. He blasted the rock. He was on fire.

He blasted the second pitch in the bottom of the first and ended up on third. DeVon singled him home with the first run. Craig patted his butt as he crossed the plate. Win, and all is forgiven. His homer in the fourth cleared Hector and Todd off the bases.

Ridgedale was leading 4–0 in the seventh when he saved Craig's shutout with a diving catch of a sinking liner over short. That got him a hug from Craig.

Slaps and shouts in the locker room. Eric Nola said, "Good job, Mak, what got into you?"

"You mean who'd he get into," said Ryan.

Everybody laughed. They knew. He swallowed the anger down. Stay cool. *BillyBuddBillyBuddBillyBudd.* Why am I still saying that?

He nodded and high-fived his way through the locker room. Coach Cody gave him a thumbs-up and a wink. *TigerbitchTigerbitchTigerbitch.*

He almost didn't notice Andy cleaning out his locker.

"What's up?"

"I'm off the team." Andy looked sad. He did care after all.

"Why?"

"Cody doesn't think I'm a positive influence." His face was so pale the freckles were reddish-brown polka dots.

"Backing me up in the cafeteria?"

Andy shrugged.

Mike lowered his voice. "Let's bring him down."

Andy shook his head. "Can't. He won."

"Only if we let him."

"Let it go."

"You want him to retain his totalitarian control of the school? Of our lives?"

Andy turned on him, his face flushing. "Don't mock me, don't . . ."

"I'm not, man. You were right. He lied about a lot of stuff. I can't just stand there anymore while he lies and lies, about Kat and Oscar, even me . . ."

"Probably lied on his résumé to get this job," said Andy.

Mike lost his breath. "You think so?"

"Be like him, wouldn't it?"

"What if we could prove that?"

Andy shrugged again. "What if we could?"

"If the school board knew that . . ."

"It's over, Mike. He can fuck us up." He zipped his bag and walked out.

Mike followed him. "You've got the balls, you . . ."

"Leave it alone." Andy didn't look at him.

"He's got something on you, too, doesn't he?" He grabbed Andy's shoulders. Andy sagged.

"Good luck." Andy's eyes glistened. "I'm sorry."

"What is it?"

"He found out it was me who turned Oscar in to Immigration."

"You? Why?"

"He shouldn't be in center field."

Mike felt nauseous. "You did it for me?"

"Partly, yeah. But why should some illegal beaner walk in and . . ."

"Okay." Mike held up his hand. He didn't want to hear this.

"I took some cell phone pictures of Oscar at school getting out of that car with New York plates. And getting picked up. I turned them in on a hotline."

"How did Coach find out?"

Andy looked down. Tears formed. "I guess I shot my mouth off."

"We'll get him," said Mike. He squeezed Andy's shoulders. "I've got another idea."

THIRTY-NINE

Zack was scared. "I'm on probation. Part of the deal was that Cody could make random checks of my hard drive."

"Sounds like steroid testing." When Zack didn't react, he said, "We'll use my computer."

"He'll check that, too."

"No, he won't. He thinks he knows everything about everybody. He thinks I'm coachable."

"What does that mean?"

"That I'll do whatever he says."

"Why are you doing this?"

It just tumbled out. "He messed with people I care about. Kat. Andy. Oscar. My dad. You."

Zack looked at him for a long time. Mike thought Zack's face was changing, eyes getting squintier, lips pressing together, even the flesh around his jaw tightening. A geek game face. Finally Zack said, "You really think we can bring him down?"

"We're the perfect team," said Mike.

"What are you talking about?"

"Pukes know how to do stuff," said Mike, "and jocks hate to lose."

They started with the copy of Coach Cody's résumé from the official website, the résumé he had submitted for the dean of discipline's job at Ridgedale High five years ago. According to the résumé, Gary James Cody was forty-eight years old. He was born in Kansas City and joined the Army after high school. Five years later he left the service as a Ranger sergeant with a Bronze star and went to Michigan State University on an Army Reserve scholarship. He played baseball there and graduated with a degree in education. He served five more years as a Ranger officer. He left the service as a captain with a Silver star and taught for ten years in various high schools in Michigan and Illinois before he was activated for a year by the Army during the Gulf War in 1990. He was wounded. Then ten years as a school administrator in Utah, Nevada, and New Hampshire before coming to Ridgedale.

Zack studied the résumé as if it were a math problem. "This is going to take a while," he said. His game face had solidified.

"What should I do?" said Mike.

"Get me spicy potato chips and A&W root beer," said

Zack. He was serious. He sounded in charge. "And gummy bears."

Mike took a deep breath. *BillyBuddTigerbitchBillyBudd*. Making a junk food run for a puke wasn't exactly what I had in mind, he thought. Suck it up, Mighty Mak. Jock keeps his eyes on the prize, does whatever he needs to win.

"Oh, and I need my tunes."

"Some Mozart while you hack?" said Mike sarcastically.

Zack didn't get it. "For this, some Fishnchip. It's on my iPhone." He dug into his dork bag.

"Fishnchip?" He dimly remembered a Canadian band Andy had listened to for a week. "Grunge?"

"No one's used that term in a decade," said Zack, and smiled.

When Mike got back from the store, Zack's eyeballs were locked onto the screen and his fingers were glued to the keyboard. He had a headset on. The cat was sitting on his lap. For a long time he didn't notice that Mike had returned or had cleared space near him for a six-pack of soda, three different bags of chips, and a sack of gummy bears.

He blinked. His fingers moved. Every so often he jerked his head and mumbled, *"'Squeeze don't pull.'"*

Mike thought of movies and TV shows he'd seen where the tough guys, heroes or villains, waited while their geek henchman, usually an Asian or black guy, but always skinny with glasses, tapped on his laptop. The tough guys would be growling, "Go, go, we've got forty seconds," and the geek would tap furiously until something popped on the screen and he'd yelp, "We're in!"

At first it was easy to follow what Zack was doing. Google, Wikipedia, Yahoo, Altavista, Technorati, then search engines that Mike had never heard of, then deep into state, federal, and military websites. Zack's head and body barely moved.

He stopped once for a can of A&W and one of the bags of chips. Two gurgles from the can and a handful of crunchies, then back to the screen. He wiped off his greasy hands on the cat. She purred. If I did that, thought Mike, she'd tear the skin off my fingers.

"Anything?" said Mike.

Zack shook his head. "So far his résumé checks out." He sagged back in the chair. The music continued to play in the background: *'Aim for the brain and squeeze don't pull'* . . . Zack rubbed his eyes and jammed a handful of gummy bears into his mouth. He locked back into the screen.

Mike heard the garage door hum up and down, car doors, his parents coming into the kitchen. It was after eleven o'clock. He locked his bedroom door and stretched out on the bed. He looked up at Billy Budd's puzzled gaze—*What are you up to, young ballers?*

Good question, Billy.

Zack was going back and forth between sides of a split screen, when he suddenly straightened up and yelped, "Game on!"

"We're in?"

"What?" Zack turned down the sound.

"What do you have?"

"He wasn't just wounded. Captain Gary James Cody was killed on January 23, 1990, in Kuwait during the Gulf War."

"That must be someone with the same name."

"Don't think so. His obit in the Kansas City Star says he was a schoolteacher in a Ranger Psych warfare unit who played baseball at Michigan State."

It took Mike a moment to get it. "Coach stole his identity!"

"Elementary, my dear Semak." Zack fell back in his chair. "Now we have to find out his real name."

"Don't people ever check out résumés?"

"Only when they want to find something."

Mom rattled his doorknob halfheartedly, as if she just wanted to go to sleep herself. Zack and Mike were still until they heard her walk away, whisper to Dad, and close their bedroom door. Too much to explain if they got caught, Mike thought.

Zack chugged an A&W and ripped open another bag of

chips. "Census," he said, logging onto a government site. "It could be someone who knew the real Cody, even grew up with him in the same town."

Zack occasionally grunted and hummed, but his thin shoulders barely moved. In the zone. He could be lifting or running through outfield drills, Mike thought. Who'd ever think pukes could concentrate like this? Why not?

His mind drifted. What was Kat doing right now in that group home? Did they let her out to run? Was she thinking about me? Cody had pushed her over the edge. To what? He remembered Lori wondering if she was bipolar. What does that actually mean? Will I ever see her again? Will she be different?

"Nothing," said Zack.

It took Mike a moment to get back to now. "Nothing?"

"Too many people around Captain Cody's age grew up with him in Kansas City. Dead end."

The poster shook its head. *Never quit, young baller.*

What would they do on *CSI*?

"Centerburg, Colorado," said Mike. "Can you see if anyone who was in Kansas City with the real Cody was also in Centerburg like twenty years ago?"

"Why?"

"Cody said he coached against Billy Budd in Little League."

"Sounds like another one of his stories," said Zack.

"Maybe not. Would you try it?"

"Might as well. You got any chocolate chip cookies?"

By the time he got back from the 7-Eleven in Nearmont, Zack was rocking in his chair, nodding and grunting. "Roger Wald. Kansas City and Centerburg. He could be the one."

"How do we find out?"

Zack smiled, leaned back, and flexed his fingers.

FORTY

The principal, Dr. Howard, made him wait a half hour in her small outer office with her stone-faced secretary, an older woman who kept shooting suspicious glances at Mike, as if she expected him to snatch the tiny glass figurines on her desktop. It would have seemed funny if he wasn't so jittery. Coach Cody could show up at any moment. He stared at Dr. Howard's closed office door, willing it to open. From behind him came the chatter and bustle of the big main office where a dozen clerks, secretaries, and volunteers, including Tori, answered phone calls, filed attendance records, and received visitors and students at the long front desk. He sensed Tori scowling at his back. He was caught in a crossfire of laser glares.

He clutched the folder and tried to practice what he was going to say, the way he had rehearsed it with Zack. Calmly. Simply. No *Law & Order* dramatics. These papers prove that the person we know as Gary James Cody is really Roger Wald. He lied on his résumé to get this job. Just lay it down, sweet as a bunt, and you'll get on base. That's all you have to do. Don't go for the home run now—time for that later. Just start the rally, get Dr. Howard on our side.

Phones rang. Period bells clanged. A bright flash of laughter from the main office. The stony secretary shook her head without looking up.

Why am I doing this? Everything's okay. I'm in center field. Captain of the team. Hitting a ton. Keep your eyes on the prize. Which is what, young baller?

Concentrate. Get back in the zone. These papers prove that the person we know as Gary James Cody is really Roger Wald. He lied on his résumé to get this job.

The door opened. Dr. Howard smiled and waved him in. He'd never been so close to her. Smaller than he thought, slimmer. Smelled good. The dark freckles on her milk-chocolate skin were kind of cute. He started to relax a little. Good. You're loose. Bad. You're getting distracted.

She shook his hand and looked up at him. "That was some catch in the Westfield Hills game. Billy Budd should see that—he'd start worrying about his job." She laughed. "Coach Cody was so proud you won that contest and so am I. What can I do for you, Mike?"

He took a breath. Get back in the zone. "These papers prove that the person we know as Gary James Cody is really Roger Wald. He lied on his résumé to get this job." He handed her the folder. "Roger Wald was never a Ranger in combat. He served two years in the Army, but all in the U.S. He was a personnel records clerk. A private. He stole a dead officer's identity."

She took the folder without opening it and nodded. "I'm glad you brought this to me, Mike. It's exactly what a captain should do." She dropped the folder on her desk. "You know, this is not the first time I've been apprised of such allegations. I was deeply concerned until we checked them out. No substance at all." She lowered her voice. "There are people out to undermine Mr. Cody and me and to turn Ridgedale High back into the unsafe, under-performing school it once was. That is simply not going to happen."

Even towering over her, Mike suddenly felt himself getting smaller, weaker, as if he had just struck out without even swinging. He struggled to control his softening muscles, deepen his voice. "That material is . . ."

"Don't tell me, Mike." She raised her hand. "I don't want to know how you got it because then I'd be forced to take action. Hacking is a federal crime, not to mention the civil lawsuits from anyone damaged by the action." She put her hand on his arm. "You've been through a lot lately, Mike, I know that, and you've handled yourself well. We were planning an assembly to celebrate your day with Billy, but that will have to wait until"—she arched her eyebrows—"your filmmaker rejoins us."

She was steering him out of her office.

He only imagined the secretary's suspicious glances turning into good-riddance dismissals, Tori's scowls into questioning looks. He was out in the hall. No way he was going to class. He ditched the day and headed for the county park.

Zack relaxed after the third time Mike swore he had not mentioned his name. "What now?"

"You've got to do better."

"Better?" His eyelids snapped open like window shades. His jaw dropped. It was almost comical. Puke's a puke, Mike thought, but he's my puke.

"I been thinking about this all day—I . . ."

"You thinking?" said Zack.

". . . figure Dr. Howard can get past the false résumé. After all, she hired him and she needs him. But anything that would tie Cody up to illegal immigration or to threatening a student with revealing her records would be just too hot. She'd flip him."

"Flip him?"

"It's a law enforcement term. Give him up. Turn him over."

Zack looked impressed. He doesn't watch crime shows, Mike thought, just science fiction. He began nodding, that toy wooden bird again dipping his beak.

"I'm going to have to bring in the hackerati."

"Hackerati?"

"The aces. Some of those On-High dot org guys."

"Can we trust them?"

Zack's eyes narrowed. "Pukes don't snitch," he said.

FORTY-ONE

Mom made her special barbecue chicken for the first time in months and got teary as Tiffany dug in. She wasn't a vegetarian anymore, and the silver hoops were gone from her eyebrows and lips, although Mike thought he could still see the holes. Dad sat back grinning. He loved having the family together.

Sophia, Tiffany, and Scotty took turns talking about their computer classes. Sophia was learning to use one in nursery school, Tiffany was taking information technology courses at a community college, and Scotty was composing chamber music on his laptop. I should introduce them to the Cyber Club, thought Mike. I've got the best computer stories, but I can't tell them here.

"I was so bummed missing you," said Tiffany. "You should've come by the restaurant."

Mom said, "When was this?"

"Mike stopped by the apartment a couple of Saturdays ago," said Tiffany.

"That was so nice," said Mom. "He never tells us anything."

"It's the age," said Tiffany. Suddenly she's so wise and old, thought Mike.

"You heard about Mike winning the Day With Billy," said Dad. "Billy's website is listing Mike's batting average these days. He's leading the team."

"Mike's captain-elect," said Mom.

"I think Sophia inherited Mike's athletic ability," said Tiffany. "She's a great Wiffle ball player."

"I hit home runs," said Sophia.

"She inherited that from me," said Dad, "not from Mike."

"Unless there's something we don't know," said Scotty.

Even Mom laughed.

Tiffany and Mom cleaned up while Dad took Sophia out on the porch for a catch. Mike followed Scotty outside so he could smoke.

"Just this week," he said apologetically, lighting up. "Calms me down."

"Must be a big competition," said Mike.

"Biggest in Europe for student string ensembles," said Scotty. "Doing well can lead to grants, jobs."

"Hope you've got a good team," said Mike. He wondered if that sounded dumb, but he felt a connection with Scotty he hadn't felt before.

"The viola is a little weak, but that's because she hasn't been with us long," said Scotty seriously. "After a while you just know what everybody else is going to do. You breathe together." He turned to blow smoke away from Mike. "I guess you're getting along with that fascist coach. What was his name?"

"Cody." He thought for a moment. Maybe Scotty has an idea. "Can you keep a secret?"

"If it's about New Jersey high school baseball, all Europe will want to know." He punched Mike's shoulder.

"Something's going down with Coach Cody. He stole a dead guy's identity to get his job."

"Are you kidding?" Scotty choked on his inhale.

"We got proof."

"What kind of proof?"

"Documents."

"What are you going to do?" Scotty looked concerned.

"I don't know. The principal blew me off. The kids who hacked the documents are trying to get more stuff, but they're staying under the radar. They're afraid of him."

"And you're not?" Scotty shook his head. "This is serious."

"No shit." He was beginning to be sorry he had brought it up.

"I mean you could go to jail for this."

"He could go to jail for this." He gave it the *CSI* edge.

"You sound like you really want to nail him."

"I do. He's a bad guy."

"World is full of them," said Scotty.

"He messed over my friends."

"Can't they take care of themselves?"

"Not all of them." He had a clear mental image of something he had never seen. Kat hanging upside down on her rack to chase the dark away. He wanted to reach out and touch her.

"You better be careful."

"Thanks." It came out more sarcastic than he had intended but Scotty let it go.

"What does Dad say?"

"Have I got a deal for you."

Scotty laughed. "That's the salesman. He's a good guy. Took me a while to see it, but he really cares about us. It's why he works so hard. He was right there with Mom getting Tiff straightened out, and he's really supported my music even though he'd rather I was in the store." Scotty rubbed out the cigarette on his sole and stuck the butt in his pocket. "Talk to him. You can trust him."

"Not about this," said Mike. "It's my problem."

Mom called them inside for dessert. Sophia was sitting on Dad's lap and Tiffany was wearing some of Mom's costume jewelry. To Mike, everybody looked flushed with contentment. He felt like he was on the other side of a window, looking in. He was glad for them, scared for himself. It's my problem.

He pretended to object when Mom and Dad insisted he stay home and get to sleep while they drove Tiffany, Sophia, and Scotty back to the city. Scotty was going to stay over with a friend before tomorrow's flight to Amsterdam. Mike could use the sleep. Big day tomorrow.

In the driveway Mike hugged Sophia and Tiffany and promised to come visit soon. Scotty pulled Mike's head down and whispered, "Give the old man a chance."

"Right," said Mike.

He didn't sleep. He visualized the meeting, Budd-style. He would stride into Cody's office, hard-faced, and before the coach could say anything slap everything Zack's hacker friends had found on his desk.

"I'm giving you a chance to resign and leave the area," he would say in a *Law & Order* mode. "Otherwise, I go to the FBI."

He'd be prepared for Coach's sneery grin, maybe even an attempt to push him out of the office. "You drunk, Semak?

You do want to graduate, don't you? Go to college?"

"Not as badly as I want you out of this school," he'd snap back. "You've got five minutes to leave, Roger Wald."

The look of terror on Cody's face, the sweat popping out of his shaven skull, was the MVP trophy he had dreamed about.

Mike, you are in some Billy Budd fantasy. Dream on. He's not going to go down that easy.

FORTY-TWO

He felt big and strong and loose in the halls. Tori looked up as he strode through the front office. "Mike!"

He ignored her and opened Cody's door.

Cody was in his friendly position, perched on a corner of his desk, talking to Nick, who was sitting in a straight chair. *That makes sense. The mole.* They looked startled as he burst in.

Don't lose the advantage.

Cody slipped off his desk into a defensive posture, balanced on the soles of his feet, open hands waist high. Mike thought of a cage fighter. "Captain Mike! Just the man I always want to see. Thanks for stopping by, Nick—you can go now."

Nick got up. "I'll check back later, Mr. Cody."

"It's Mr. Wald," said Mike. He felt warm, zoned. "His real name is Roger Wald. Stick around, Nick, the FBI is going to be interested in you, too."

Cody laughed. "Don't tell me you got caught in that scam, too, Mike. It's old news. Must be Zack the Hack. Look, I don't want to press criminal and civil charges against Berger and his family, but if this keeps cropping up I'll have no choice. And against you, too."

Mike dropped a sheaf of papers on Cody's desk. "Then there's the emails between you and the *buscones*. We had to get some of them translated. I was surprised you were getting a piece of the action if any of their players got pro contracts."

Cody snatched the papers, began tearing them up. "I'm doing you a favor, Mike. You could go to jail for this."

"Unless I get a whistleblower's reward from Homeland Security. Falsifying information on the status of an immigrant is pretty serious."

"Don't try to bluff me," said Cody.

Nick hadn't left. He said, "Those geeks can put anything all over the world in a minute."

Cody said to Mike, "What do you want?"

"I want you gone."

Cody's big muscles went into tremors under his white shirt. "What's this about? That nutty slut you hooked up with?"

BillyBuddBillyBuddBillyBudd. He was surprised to be

hearing that name in his head. Why not? It was Billy who got me this far. "You messed over a lot of people in this school."

"I kept this school secure."

"From what?"

"You stupid punk," said Cody. "Good men die so you and your candy-ass friends can play ball, screw your brains out, repeat any kind of dumb bullshit that makes you feel hip. It's a mean world out there, gangbangers and drug pushers and terrorists, and I've kept them out of this school. Kept you safe."

"Kept us under your thumb."

"Who told you that? Your big-mouth pal Andy Baughman who sent Oscar Ramirez and his dad back to the Dominican Republic?"

Nick snickered. Cody shot him a triumphant look and rocked back on his heels.

"It doesn't take much pressure to make losers fold. Zack and those pukes settled pretty fast, your head case Tigerbitch couldn't wait to run away, and you were all set to snitch, weren't you?"

I don't know, Mike thought. He remembered how numb and nervous he had felt that Monday morning, unsure what he was going to say if Cody pulled him out of class to grill him about the Saturday trip into the city with the Cyber Club. Was he set to snitch? He never found out. Nick beat him to it.

Cody bellowed, "I said, 'weren't you?'"

Cody seemed to grow taller, expand, loom over him. The office was hot, it was hard to breathe. He felt small and weak. What made him think he could pull this off? Should have listened to Andy: *"He won. Leave it alone."*

"You better leave now," said Cody. "Before I press charges. You plan on coming back to school, you better bring your dad along." He snickered. "Mister Dealmaker."

"Mister Dealmaker. I like that. Might put it up in the store."

Mike whirled. Dad was standing in the doorway, smiling, hands in his pockets. He looked relaxed. Cool. Behind him, Tori and the office staff were trying to peer over his broad shoulders.

"What the hell you want?"

Dad's hands came out of his pockets, opened, palms up, so here's the deal. "Thought I could help out before anyone has to go to the police. Of course, for all I know, identity theft, impersonation, lying on federal documents, could be matters for the FBI, Homeland Security. I'm just a flooring salesman."

Nick was on his hands and knees, looking at the papers Cody had torn and thrown on the floor. "There are official files here."

"They hacked it," said Cody. "People are afraid of nukes

in suitcases. They should be scared shitless of pukes online."
His eyes were wild. "The next terrorist strike is going to
come from cyberspace, shutting down everything, light,
heat, air traffic, defense systems . . ."

Nick was waving the torn papers. "This true?" The web
on his neck seemed to be quivering.

"It's true," said Mike. "He's a con man."

"Conned me, too," said Nick. He was almost babbling. "Promised to keep me out of jail if I snitched for
him."

"You little junkie," yelled Cody, aiming a kick at Nick,
who scrambled out of the way. "I'll have you back in juve-
nile hall for knocking Mike off his bike."

"What was that about?" said Dad.

"I'm sorry, Mike," said Nick, "I was trying to cover my
ass, make the pukes think it was you ratted them out."

"Endangering minors," said Dad. "That's for the local
cops. The chief's my customer. You're done here, Cody."

Cody said, "You're making a big mistake, Semak. Your
kid'll go down with this."

"You heard my dad," said Mike. He felt big and hard.
"You're done."

Cody turned on Mike. "I put you on the varsity, Semak."
He was sweating. "I put you in center field. Made you the
captain. Why are you doing this to me?"

Mike thought, Because it's what I thought Billy Budd would do. Is that a reason?

"What's going on here?" Dr. Howard had pushed past Dad into the room.

"I'm not going to let them turn this school into a circus." Cody stuffed papers into a briefcase. "But you can bet I'll be back and you will all be in the worst trouble of your life."

Mike got out of his way as Cody charged through the office, shouldering past Dr. Howard and Dad, out his door, scattering the staff.

Mike felt exhausted. A little scared. What's next?

"How about some breakfast?" said Dad. "Didn't get a chance this morning." He was smiling, rubbing his hands together.

Mike was glad to see Dad's hands were trembling, too.

FORTY-THREE

He felt the springy green grass and soft earth under his spikes, the June sun cooking the hairs on the back of his neck. He took a deep breath and closed his eyes to hold the moment. He remembered visualizing this day back in March, before the season began, a lifetime ago, before Kat and Oscar and Zack, when Cody was the coach and Billy Budd was a mythical creature on his screen and on his wall.

"Yo, Mak." Ryan, trotting out to right field, lobbed a soft toss. Mike caught it, turned, and lobbed it to Eric Nola in left, who made the long throw over Mike's head to Ryan. He had wondered if he and Ryan would ever be best friends again, if he even wanted to be, but after a while they had drifted back together, throwing soft punches and wisecracks, and he realized that their friendship was long but not deep, and that was okay, too. He was glad Andy had rejoined the team. As captain, Mike could use a wingman with a big mouth.

Craig finished his warm-ups and stood impatiently on the mound as Coach Sherman, Jimmy Russo, and the infield gathered around to calm him down. Of all the seniors, Craig had taken Coach Cody's sudden disappearance hardest. He lost his swaggering confidence for a while, as if he had gotten it from Cody. He wasn't the only one who expected Cody to show up one day, in camo, armed, to clean up the school. But as weeks passed and the cops and the counselors assured everyone that Cody was gone for good, Craig's fastball started cooking again. Still, he was tight and jittery before a game. Who wasn't?

Mike rechecked the flag moving gently above the scoreboard. The light breeze was still blowing in. Fly balls would hang. Need to play even shallower than usual.

The band struck up the school song and the cheerleaders began a tumbling routine. Lori and Tori twirled. They still weren't talking to Mike, but Lori had given him a tight smile as they passed in the hall today. He felt sorry for Lori although her suffering act was getting old. Ryan said if he groveled just a little he could hook up with her again, but what was the point? You can't go backward.

The meeting at the mound broke up and Coach Sherman yelled, "Shake your eyeballs, Rangers." When he took over there was talk about changing the nickname back to

Ridgerunners but the school board didn't want to pay for fixing the scoreboard and the uniforms. Maybe next year. He wondered if Cody was keeping up with the team, wherever he was. He was a good coach, Mike thought, and he brought me up to the varsity. But he was a bad guy. The local police and a woman from the FBI had talked to him, but not all that much, and it was not as exciting as *CSI*. Dad said the school and the town wanted to keep it all as quiet as possible. There was a notice that Cody had left for "personal" reasons.

Wonder what Oscar's doing back in the DR. Maybe he's already sneaked back into the country to play at some other high school. Be great to see his name on a major league roster someday. Imagine if he signed with the Yankees, pushed Billy Budd to left field. Of course, not the way Billy's playing this season. We're burning up our leagues together again.

He scanned the stands until he found the Mike Semak section. Mom and Dad were waving. They had even less time now with both stores open, but they made at least a few innings of his home games. Love to see them here, but I'd understand if they didn't show. They've always been there when we needed them, Scotty was right about that. And Scotty was right to tell Dad about Coach Cody. Couldn't have done it alone. Still get chills thinking about

Dad walking into Coach's office like in the closing minutes of *Law & Order*. Scotty loved hearing that, cheered him up. His ensemble did okay in Amsterdam but they didn't win. The viola. Next time.

Zack and the Cyber Club were sitting behind Mom and Dad cheering for him. Josh and Tyler were there, although he still wasn't sure which was which. Some of the old folks, including Regina Marie. He promised to go back to the senior center after the season. Teach them how to hack. That got a laugh from Zack.

On RidgedaleReform.org he'd read that Nick had been spotted buying a beer in a Nearmont bar just before it was busted for serving underage kids. He was narking again for the local police. Need to catch up to him one of these days. Not such a bad guy.

Time to get your head in the game.

Easy, Mak, you've got a minute. You can't enjoy the now unless you remember the then. Who said that? You did.

Not bad for a dumb jock. Remember to tell Kat that one. She said she'd call after the game. I finally have a reason to leave my cell on, especially at night when she has time to call. Lots of activities and meetings and therapy sessions in that group home. With every call her voice sounds lighter, clearer. He could tell she was as happy to hear his voice as he was to hear hers. She was taking less medicine, she said, and coming to better understand Kat and Tigerbitch. She might be back for a visit this summer. His body flushed at the thought.

He'd never talked so much to another human being as he talked to Kat late at night. She loved to hear about him and Zack teaming up to bring down Cody. Made him tell that story over and over. She always howled with laughter at his junk food runs for Zack, and the first couple of times he described the final scene in Cody's office she started sniffling when Dad showed up.

And she loved to hear about the first times he had watched the video that won the Billy Budd contest, how his own focus had slowly widened until he saw all the other people in the room.

He tried to talk about what had happened inside him since that March afternoon in the boys' locker room, how he had changed, but he just wasn't ready yet. Maybe he was saving that for when they were together again.

Okay, Mak, drill down. Game time.

The first batter strutted to the plate. Right-hander, a pull hitter according to scouting reports. Mike waved Eric closer to the left field foul line and signaled Ryan to take a few steps in.

He zoned in, hummed to himself, *We're born again, there's new grass on the field.*